# Psychomachia

# Psychomachia

Sanita Fejzić

The publication of *Psychomachia* has been generously supported by the Canada Council for the Arts and the Ontario Arts Council.

Author's photograph: Phillip Mirsky
Cover painting: Mathieu Laca, *Judith*, 2015
Cover design: Natasha Shaikh
Typography: Zile Liepins
Editor: Anne Cunningham

Library and Archives Canada Cataloguing in Publication

Fejzić, Sanita, author
Psychomachia / Sanita Fejzić.

ISBN 978-1-988254-26-5 (paperback)

I. Title.

PS8611.E455P79 2016 C813'.6 C2016-905885-9

Published by Quattro Books Inc.
Toronto
quattrobooks.ca

Printed in Canada

*The Ottawa Magazine*
*February 10, 2011*

**No Rest for Anne Dumont-Belović's Parents**

After facing an alleged sexual assault at the age of 16 by four boys and being subsequently bullied, 18-year-old Anne Dumont-Belović committed suicide last month. We caught up with her parents to see how they're coping with the loss.

Gabriel Dumont, winner of the 2010 Governor General's Literary Award for his debut book of poetry, *Back Entry*, said his daughter was never the same after the dreadful evening the four boys sexually assaulted her.

After one of the boys posted a cellphone picture of the alleged sexual assault on Facebook, Anne Dumont-Belović was bullied online and in her high school in downtown Ottawa. She dropped out of school a month later, and eventually committed suicide after being diagnosed with post-traumatic stress disorder, depression and anxiety.

Her mother, Judith Belović, one of Canada's most celebrated architects, has been silent since the start of the case. She declined to be interviewed.

Dumont, outraged by the RCMP's handling of his daughter's allegations of sexual assault, which resulted in no criminal charges, demanded a review of the case in a lengthy Facebook post. Dumont wrote:

> We lost our daughter to suicide last week because four boys thought they could get away with sexually assaulting her. Loss opens the mind to new spaces, new states of being, where everything is suddenly steeped in doubt. Borders are broken by brute force. New ideas emerge from sombrous corners while others are ripped out by the roots.

> I question authority. I explode my inner boundaries. This is survival.
>
> Our wounds gape open in apposition and opposition, and we face each other across empty rooms, virtual pages, from coast to coast, asking, begging, waiting for justice.
>
> We live in antiphony. We defy spiritual atrophy.
>
> We become the cacophony of loss. Grief is the new language we speak and its words have started to define us. Its emptiness threatens our sanity.
>
> We demand a review of the case: we demand truth, integrity and due process for our only child. The law, which is meant to protect victims and uphold justice, has failed us. What kind of precedent does this set?
>
> The brutality of our loss has blurred the boundary between the personal and the public. Our intimate lives have made national headlines. While the whole country mourns our loss – while politicians and journalists debate – our hearts bleed with unresolved pain.

When asked if the "we" in his note referred to him and his wife, Dumont's eyes emptied of all emotion. His wife, he said, is shaken and has taken a year off work.

She was the lead architect on a new wing for the Canadian Museum of Nature but has abandoned the project due to current circumstances. Her vision – the kind of structural *tour de force* we have learned to expect from her – was to build upon the museum's original architecture in striking new ways.

In an earlier statement, she said, "David Ewart [the museum's original architect] created a fancy, castle-like structure in a Scottish Baronial style. Growing up in Croatia and travelling the continent, I am of course very sensitive to this aesthetic. My minimalist approach will complement his heavy, dense tastes."

Belović added, "I will honour the history but not be burdened by its limitations. I want to make it fresh. Yes, I want to ground the new structure in the present reality of Canada."

When asked what that present reality was, Belović was as silent as she has been since the death of her daughter.

Canada grieves with the Dumont-Belović family. The couple, a cultural powerhouse, has gained momentum for their cause and support from a number of organizations, associations and MPs, who are pressuring the government to take action on violence against women and the current lack of cyberbullying laws.

# One

*Time passes. Moments roll into one another. You tilt your head sideways and look out the framed window. A snow-white spider has woven a web and is walking along the thin, silky arteries toward its prey. A honeybee, dead and waiting. You know dead things cannot wait. Surely, the dead are outside the web of time, in a space where the verb "wait" has no meaning. Or maybe not. You are certain of nothing except the thing you can see: a spider is about to eat the insect it has caught in its web. You turn your head. You think you could never corner and kill an innocent being like that. But something compels you to look again and witness the dimpled spider, fat and fast, pull on the string like a wizard shaking his wand before proceeding toward its prey. Its front legs almost touch the dead insect before it suddenly starts to produce more of the smooth fibre from its rear end. You are fascinated as it masterfully wraps the dead insect in silk, as if a mother were wrapping her baby tight in a white cotton cloth. Fast and helpless, the bee's body spins around as if caught in a witch's spinning wheel. Satisfied, the spider's fangs dig into the bee's body. Head shaking, you turn your back on the grim scene.*

She is late again this morning and knows it. She strokes her blouse in front of the mirror, fingers gripping buttons with practiced force and yet, somehow, uncertain about their next move.

*You weren't always this way.*

The woman in the reflection only appears to be like her. Her eyes are black, made even blacker by the thick mascara and eyeliner. No amount of makeup can cover up the fatigue on her face.

She hasn't slept properly in years.

Everything is stainless steel in the kitchen. The toaster. The fridge. The oven. Yes, even the dish rack.

The sound the toaster makes when the bread pops out startles her. It doesn't have to be alive for her to know its intentions. It's in the air. Maybe she's losing her mind, thinking the toaster is threatening. But then again, one never knows. Machines pulse with electrical energies in much the same way we do.

She unplugs the toaster and picks up the slice of bread.

Every time she has to bend over to reach for the butter in the fridge, her lower back aches. It would be more accurate to say *almost* every time. Not always. Her mind, however, is attached to the memories of pain, and she can barely recall the times she took out the butter without suffering at least a little bit. She's getting old, she tells herself. At forty-three.

No, she's not. But she likes to tell herself she is. The stories she tells herself are alluring and somehow lulling, and serve a purpose she can't entirely know. Perhaps to distract her but she would resist that thought. Judith doesn't see herself as the kind of woman prone to distractions.

A blackbird lands in her backyard, past the spider web, past the porch. There are at least thirteen ways she could look at the bird, but she interprets its eyes as reflections of her own. A woman and a blackbird are one. Just in the same way, she thinks, a woman and her past are one. When Anne was four years old, she used to give blackbirds food, which Gabriel had warned her not to do. He was superstitious, believed the birds to be bearers of bad luck. But Judith remembers the gratitude the birds expressed towards her daughter, bringing her buttons and pins, and other gifts. She rubs her eyes, as if trying to let go of the memory. She has to focus on the present moment. On getting to work on time for once.

In the cabinet with stainless steel handles, she reaches for an unopened jar of strawberry jam, her favourite. Once again, her hands, firm around the lid, seem to waver. "Come on," she commands. *Come on, now.*

She remembers a trick her father taught her. She picks out a butter knife, perfectly shined, from her kitchen drawer. She looks at its round blade for a moment. Why has she taken it out? The confusion does not last long. She remembers the jam and the toast, and her father's trick. She wonders how much time she spends being confused in a given day. There is no way of knowing unless she becomes meticulous about it and starts to measure time.

But she has an aversion to measuring things, particularly time. She considers this aversion a part of her very being, having decided to build her identity on it at some point in her life, maybe in childhood or maybe later on. She could not change it now. It would destabilize who she was. Who she is.

The lid comes right off after she uses the knife as a lever.

"That was easy," she says.

Sometimes she speaks out loud like that, to some second or third person inside of her. Sometimes there are entire conversations inside of her, and God only knows which one of these voices is actually her. Maybe she is a collection of voices.

Spreading the butter is not a challenge, even though it's hard and crumbly from being in the fridge. She wonders why, after she and Gabriel divorced, she didn't continue in their habit of leaving butter out on the counter so it would be easy to spread. It doesn't matter. Habits live and die, as do all things. Just like her marriage, which ended when Judith became hard as a brick.

The death of their daughter had changed Gabriel. He went from being a poet looking for beauty, converting unexpected moments into works of art, to an angry man with a mission. His metamorphosis disturbed her. He put down his pen and paper and started to carry protest posters in front of Parliament. Like a madman, he stood in rain and snow, alone or accompanied by a few others, screaming for justice. He stopped shaving; God, he neglected his personal hygiene to the point of Judith having to remind him to shower. He reeked of anger and thoughts of revenge changed the shape of his eyes. They grew big with the desire for retribution. It was as if he fed off the media attention, like a vampire, as if he had gone from being a loving father and husband to a fanatic spokesperson against cyberbullying. She couldn't recognize him. Her need for privacy was violated left, right and centre – why couldn't her husband understand that and honour it? In the rare moments when Gabriel's eyes regained their lost lustre, when he turned to hold her at night, expressing feelings of sorrow and grief and coupling them with hope and love, she felt her body go numb. His humanity was more painful than his acrimony.

When he was hard with desire for her, it was as if an unwelcome, solid rod of iron ripped through her. She was reminded of her daughter's rape, the word made her nauseous, the thought of Anne's suicide choked her, and she could do nothing but push Gabriel away, drive him over the edge, blame him for washing their most delicate, precious linen in public until he erupted with irony which she met with silence, which never failed to awaken his rage; until Judith's skin grew so thick as to become inaccessible to her husband; until finally, worn out and disheartened, she asked for a divorce, severing herself from the man whose face constantly reminded her of her dead daughter, the only man she had truly loved – that is, when she was capable of feeling such emotions as love.

Memories have physiological effects on the body. Judith's heart beats in her neck, which is tense, as if trying to defend itself against the past.

She sits at the kitchen table, looking out the window. She chews slower than necessary. The toast is too hard. The toaster over-toasted her bread – that damned thing. Is this proof of the toaster's maleficence? Or is this a self-fulfilling prophecy, where she assigns meaning to something only to reassure herself that her suspicions were right? She should feel something about this, but doesn't. Her mouth is at a left-angle slant, lips sealed, as if refusing to eat.

She wills herself to finish the toast anyway, because this is what you do in the morning to have a good life: you eat breakfast.

It strikes her only at this moment that she has forgotten about the coffee.

Outside the window, she sees movement from the corner of her eye. Maybe the blackbird, but no, it wasn't black and it wasn't a bird. The empty backyard gives no further clues and her mind, trying to replay the moment, thinks it was probably a stray cat, but maybe not. If it was a cat, it was an orange one. If it wasn't a cat, then she's not sure about the colour. How could that be?

She notices the sky outside. The atmosphere of the day enters her being. Grey and windy. The clouds, frothy like polluted ocean foam, hold their backs to her. Summer, so slow to come, has arrived grumpy.

Her BlackBerry rings as the water boils.

She follows the sound into the living room, which is bare of the kind of furniture you'd expect. No sofa or table, no lamps or bookshelves. There is a single chair and a blank canvas on an easel, facing away from the window. The unopened box of paint sits by the leg of the easel, collecting dust. The blinds are drawn, and the rays of light that strike and scrape the walls enchant the room with a dim haze. The BlackBerry is on the chair, where she left it last night.

"Yes?" This is not a question even though it sounds like one.

She knows Shannon, her business partner, is on the other line. No one else calls.

"Where are you?"

"The coffee, I forgot about the coffee."

"You have to be in Montréal for eleven. I can't take care of the intern. You have to take him."

She's back in the kitchen. The kettle whistles.

"Hello?"

"Hello."

"Judith," says Shannon, emphasising the "th". Judith likes the way Shannon says her name, reminding her of who she is. "You remember what's today, right?"

Memory is a strange thing made of layers, of blanks and locked doors. It is the mind's record of moments, hopefully stacked in chronological order like a neat deck of cards. Sometimes memory is like the line of a poem, possibly fictional and filled with literary devices, and yet it has the capacity to touch the truth better than if it were filmed on camera, with an objective lens and no edits.

"Forgot my coffee," she repeats.

"Don't forget the intern. You *have* to come by the office before you go. I can't leave him here alone. It's his first day."

Shannon is the organized one, they both know this. What does that make Judith? She is the artist. The architect. Shannon is her business partner, the one that calls her to remind her of important things. Things like the intern.

"Do I have to bring him with me?"

"Yes, honey. It's his first day. He's waiting for ya. I'm waiting for ya. When will you be in? I have to leave, like, five minutes ago."

What would it mean to leave five minutes ago? She visualizes two Shannons who simultaneously coexist in two parallel universes, one leaving five minutes ago and the other speaking to her on the phone right now, vaguely aware of the other Shannon, just as we are all vaguely aware of our own shadows.

The stainless steel Bodum is nowhere to be found. She recalls the sentence written on the practical little coffee maker: "The fresh way to brew fresh coffee & tea." Why is this seemingly useless information the kind of thing Judith can remember?

BlackBerry still in her hand, she opens her Instagram feed as she goes through the cabinets and drawers, looking for the Bodum. Sworn off all other social media (she is not a social person, however you stretch the definition of the words), she spends hours, sometimes entire nights, on Instagram. Follows street artists and urban poets. Scribblers. The ones who, like criminals, crawl out of street corners at night and (spray)paint walls. Something about their clandestine nature. No, not that. Something about their impulse to express art in places that aren't meant for it, on buildings and bridges that are guarded off as public domain. The boundary between public and private blurred – yes, that's what fascinates her ...

That's why the phone was on the chair. She spent the night looking at the feed of an anonymous street artist from Buenos Aires, @andandor. He posts at least fifty images per day. He has over eight thousand posts in total: some of his process, some of his finished work. Never of himself. He does Photoshop, sculpture and street art, and collage on paper, wood, and cardboard. They are all connected by a common element: body parts. Parts that are of an indeterminate, unseen, decentralized whole yet somehow unified. Half seen, half missing. As if he attempts to capture a human being and then abandons the process, or loses the will. Maybe not abandons. He paints a nose and an eye, then leaves a blank space, and then the colour blue. Maybe that is the only way to paint a person.

She finds the Bodum and then opens the Calendar app on her phone. Montréal, 11 a.m. She is meeting with the mayor and his councillors, pitching her proposal for a new contemporary art museum by the docks, refurbishing an old flour factory that's been vacant for decades. She likes empty things that are of no use. She finds their potential for figurative meaning to her taste.

In front of the mirror again, she sees something dead in those black eyes in the reflection. Each time she looks in this mirror, she sees a new woman. There is no consistency in mirrors; she cannot trust them.

She must be back for 7 p.m. for her shooting lessons at the gun club and should leave Montréal before 1 p.m. if she is to avoid Ottawa's rush-hour traffic. She hates being stuck and waiting. She hates being stuck and waiting, and what else? The club's range conducting officer – *what's his name* – insists on timeliness. He says that you can judge a person by their relationship to time.

Now, the woman in the mirror looks worried. Scared, almost. Or perhaps terrified by the promise of pleasure. Anticipating the pistol in her hand moulds and reshapes her face. Beneath the fear, she has the look of a woman who just drank a cup of coffee and found a precious gem at the bottom. Beneath that mask is another, and beneath it, something dark and deadening. She glimpses at her clenched jaw, the hard contours of her face, and looks away.

She runs up the stairs. Slows down halfway, afraid to spill the coffee.

Her bedroom is much like her living room, bare and impersonal. She stops at the threshold, breathing heavily. For a brief moment, she is a stranger in her own house. Whose bed is that? Bedsheets tucked in neatly. The hardwood creaks as she walks to the night table. She hears her footsteps in delay. It's as if the sound is slow to travel to her ears. In the drawer, her pistol. The Smith & Wesson: a stainless-steel framed, single-action, semi-automatic pistol. The SW1911, black and perfectly moulded to her hand. Or at least that's what she thinks.

When she holds it, it's as if she is one with the machine. As if it were an extension of her self. When she holds it, it is beautiful, black and rigid, of the kind of beauty that eludes the rational mind. She is connected to it not physically, not emotionally, but spiritually. She's powerful. She has power, yes, is empowered, and filled with threatening potential.

The earplugs and earmuffs are in the drawer below, but the pistol's case is missing.

And she's late again this morning, she knows it.

*You weren't always this way, losing things, forgetting and remembering, always caught in the process of forgetting and remembering. You were once a different woman, whole and knowing. Not second-guessing and maybe-ing, no. There was constancy or at least the pretence of it. Your identity, though it always moved like a wave, was a vast ocean. Even if the waves crashed rocky shores with the full force of a storm, it never changed the essence of the ocean. Below its surface, in the depths, you always sensed calm waters. There was less confusion. Less doubt, too. This doubt, which led you to buy the SW1911 in the first place, from fear of being attacked. For the possibility of annihilating any predator, should he dare face you. God! If only Anne could have defended herself. If only you had been there.*

His name is Claude, the range conducting officer. The triumph of remembering his name, a small victory in the emptiness of her room, causes her to shriek. She smiles. She remembers the words Claude repeats every Tuesday and Thursday night at shooting practice: power, precision and speed. You see, look: shooting is a sport. Power, precision and speed are qualities that can be studied and excelled at.

She gives up on finding the pistol case. The gun slides silently into her large purse beside the BlackBerry. She does not realize that she has forgotten the earplugs and earmuffs.

# Two

The clouds are low and grey. As Judith locks the front door, her trench coat lifts and a cold breeze drifts up her legs. She shivers. The walkway from her door to the garage lane is made of red bricks. It winds around her yard and is lined with flowers, green stems with yellow and purple petals that look severely neglected. Squinting, she tries to remember the names of the flowers, making a mental note to take better care of them. She wants to see their colour and vitality in full bloom this year; it's time, she thinks, for their beauty to grace her front yard. Judith has three old trees, one oak and two maples, with a patchwork of hostas underneath. Together, they make the whole house seem lush with life.

An odd sound competes with the click of her flat shoes and distracts her from her mental endeavours. She recognizes a human voice and turns her head. He moans louder to attract her attention. Seeing him with arms spread apart like a fallen Jesus, crushing her hostas, she instinctively tightens the belt around her waist and firmly squeezes the large straps of her purse, which is at the risk of falling from her shoulder.

His fingers move. He's awake. He lowers and raises his lashes slowly. She knows that gentle blinking, that intimate invitation, and remembers in that very instant a scene when Anne was a toddler and Gabriel played with her in their old backyard, rolling around and pretending he was a puppy. He used to make Anne laugh. *He used to make you laugh.* She resists the part of herself that wants to run to his rescue.

When a blue minivan drives by, she feels suddenly exposed, as if someone were peeking inside her bathroom window while she showered. She does not want her neighbours to see him this way. The unanticipated memory of the countless reporters that showed up to their home and on the steps of her office, with camera lights flashing in her eyes and blinding her, provokes in Judith a fear of someone unexpectedly recording this scene and then airing it on the 6 o'clock news across the entire nation, for psychologists to pitch in with their perspectives, not to mention cultural critics, politicians and regular citizens, too. She remembers, with dread, the prime minister's response to Anne's suicide – his promise to erect new laws in defence of victims of cyberbullying.

Judith places a hand on her chest, trying to keep her anxiety in check. He raises himself onto all fours and crawls toward her, like a toddler. It's humiliating to watch. She can bear it no longer. Her body moves.

She jumps over the sick flowers and paces toward him. Her shoes become moist and her feet cold. She sighs in irritation.

"What are you doing here?" she says, accusing him, when her legs are a few inches away from his nose. Both hands now grip the purse straps. She uses the bag as a shield – it's black and big and hangs between him and her. Will remain between them when and if he stands and towers over her.

"Gabriel," she says, in a low but forceful voice. "You have to leave." She looks around the street. "Please leave."

He laughs one of those desperate laughs that is meant to move Judith but whose effect creates the opposite in her, hardening her skin and bones.

She lowers herself to his level. The purse is squeezed between her chest and knees. The hard frame of the gun presses against her breasts, and the feeling scares and reassures her at once.

His green eyes are magnificent even when they're completely wasted. *How could that be?*

He smells like nachos and alcohol. Vodka. Or maybe some other liquor. Something strong. He wasn't a drinker before. She is both disgusted and concerned. Because of her damn position, she feels her heart hammering against the leather bag. She sees herself reflected in his eyes, her face round and disproportionately larger than the rest of her body.

"I just came by to say hi," he mutters. His voice is pleading.

She knows the way his eyebrows curl when he lies.

"Hi."

He laughs and she moves back. Is it vomit she smells? There are no stains on his brown t-shirt other than damp soil patches. Seeing his goosebumps, she feels suddenly cold.

He tells her he's sorry. He's been sorry for the last two years, since the divorce. She notices he still wears his wedding ring. A combative part of her is awakened and she's angry again. She wants him to leave as soon as possible.

"I have to go," she says. "I'm late for work."

He tries to hold her, but she's more agile than him.

When he says he loves her still, he crosses an invisible barrier, a point of no return. When he says he wants to try and have another child even though, yes, they're in their early forties and it's a crazy idea, he's talking to another woman. Not the Judith from five minutes ago, the woman who closed the door and began to walk toward her car, but another Judy, one that's more like a warrior than an architect, one that's savage and wild, not the Judith that was domesticated for two decades and bore a child with this man.

She lifts her upper body and looks down on him resentfully. Gabriel is still on all fours as she kneels by him. He is aware of the shift in her, she can tell by the sorry look on his face. The change is energetic, unseen by the naked eye. It is felt. Discovered.

She opens her purse and takes out her wallet, which is far from the pistol. A one-hundred dollar bill is all she has. She considers the implications of this little piece of plastic paper with the face of Robert Borden. Something about his moustache arrests her and she spends a few seconds too long looking at the photo of the dead prime minister.

Gabriel is on his knees, echoing the posture in which he proposed to her. No, she does not want to be reminded of this image, this memory. He proposed to her after they found out she was pregnant. Gabriel is like that. He is the kind of man who sees symbolic meaning in everything. Even now, she knows, he's imagining their encounter to be filled with layers of meaning that she does not agree with. Before he can speak, she hands him the bill.

"What?"

"For a taxi," she says.

The hurt on his face strains her. As if she will be held responsible for her action later. He crumples the bill and throws it back at her. It falls to the ground. Her lips tighten.

Guilt, for her, is like an inner signal, telling her something has to change. As if pressing a rewind button, she picks up the bill and puts it back in her wallet. She feels drained of her vitality.

The man changes before her. This man whom she loved – maybe still loves? – for most of her adult life, this man with a dirty t-shirt and wet jeans who had slept by her house after stumbling over from the pub ... his face is changing. He compresses his lips and moves his chin forward. He stares at her with hostile eyes, furrowed brows and a wrinkled forehead.

"You're a wall," he yells. "You built this wall of unforgiveness, with blocks of titanium, keeping me out, cursing our marriage, and for what? You think the fortress will keep Anne's loss at bay? You've only jailed yourself in the past and you know it."

She closes her eyes.

"You're cruel," he says, without much conviction. His voice is jeopardized by a mixture of unbearable sorrow and anger. His face reddens and he points at her, moving his index finger about like a sword. "There is no love, there is no intensity of emotion worth living for that doesn't come at the risk of fierce pain or, at the extreme end of the spectrum, the possibility of loss, of death. You've not lost me – I'm here, Judith, and I love you."

He speaks so rapidly, it's hard to keep up with him. She opens her eyes wide in mock amazement.

"Well, it's good to see you can get piss drunk, sleep on my lawn, and then wake up with one-hundred percent clear perception, yelling and waking up my neighbours."

He reacts to her with an intense glare. Then, lifting his shoulders up quickly, he says, voice wavering, "Don't be so hard on me, Judy. Please."

"No, of course not," she responds, unable to hide the bitterness. "Thank you very much for yelling at me." She wipes some of his spit from her cheek, purses her lips and forces a smile for added effect. "I'm not sure what your dinner consisted of last night. Was it vodka or something else? The nachos I'm sure about, but the vodka is fifty-fifty."

She locks her jaw and gives him that smile again.

"You don't care about anything or anyone," he articulates slowly, his nose a few inches away from her own.

She is aware that he is not talking about this moment. He's not accusing her for what's happening right now. He's referring to what happened four years ago, when their daughter died. She knows that he's still angry that she filed for divorce. He was often like this when they met, using a present situation to express residual feelings from the past. She was annoyed and tired of the melodrama, but no matter what she did, whether she resisted him, ignored him, or was kind to him, he kept coming back to her, never wavering in his persistence.

In a way, they were stuck, like two mad people in one straitjacket, struggling to wiggle themselves out of the tension, heat and discomfort. Note the determiner "a" in "a way." It's vague, this insight, and could be misguided.

She considers her options.

To continue talking to him would be a form of suicide, would it not? She feels as though one part of her is asking this question to another. The first woman, the one who would save him, is still in love with Gabriel. The second woman, the one who took out the hundred-dollar bill, hates him in a razor-sharp, clean way. The question is: who would have to die in order to stay here with Gabriel? The first or the second woman?

He says, "You were bound to me."

*After so much kneeling, you finally stand. You're not going to listen to this emotional blackmail anymore.* He follows her, obviously determined. The purse doesn't do much to shield her from Gabriel. He is a foot taller than her and much, much wider.

"You *are* bound to me," he says, as if the change in verb tense has the force to produce an effect that cannot be denied. She reaches into the purse. His brows flex in a way she does not understand. She takes the BlackBerry out of its case.

"Do you want me to call a taxi, an ambulance or the police?" she says. "It's your choice. I have no preference."

Above, the clouds have formed two thick, dark lines approaching one another, like brigades. A handful of blackbirds fly in an arc, blurring into black dots as they leave her field of vision. The hurt on his face, once again. This time, the wound is deeper. He takes a step back and lowers his head slightly. His mouth gapes, and he breathes heavily, gravely, as if he'd just been punched in the gut. She tries to pretend not to notice, but it's not easy. The woman inside her that's still in love with Gabriel is aching at the look of his pale face. Judith has to work hard at managing this woman. Somehow, she hasn't aged, is stunted to a time before Anne's death, perhaps even before Anne's birth, when things were simple and carefree.

He tries to hug her and almost succeeds. This shakes her foundation, makes her weak at the knees. Gabriel is still handsome, as bearded and unstable as he may be. Why is she having these thoughts?

*You can do this. You can walk away from him. Just turn around and take one step toward the car, then another, then another. It's that easy.*

Oh, how complex and devastating are certain decisions.

He does not try to hold her back. Maybe she would have wavered if he had tried.

She feels unsteady and unreliable as she starts the car. Maybe he's right. Maybe she's changed so much she doesn't know who she really is. Was she ever anyone, specifically?

She sees him from the rear-view mirror, walking away. She avoids her reflection, does not yet want to decide which woman inside her needs attention the most. The one that loves him: she's crying. The one that hates him: she's crying, too.

# Three

She turns the car on and the GPS welcomes her, says, "Hello," in a woman's voice. Judith turns it off and sighs, biting her upper lip.

She turns left when she should have turned right, to avoid driving past him. Then the BlackBerry rings with that horrible piercing sound that knifes through her skin and settles in her bones, shaking them.

*Shannon. She's going to kill you; you're so late it's absurd.*

And then it comes to her: the names of those yellow and purple flowers that line her path and that have yet to fully blossom this season, even though it's mid-July already. The purple ones with the large petals and black centres that grow on strong stems are called black-eyed Susans. Also known as echinacea. Or maybe not. No, definitely not echinacea. She blows her nose one last time, and has stopped crying. The others, whose yellow, daisy-like flowers that should bloom all summer long and can make beautiful bouquets for family and friends, they're commonly called tickseed. She can't remember their Latin name. It'll come to her when she doesn't need the information, she's sure of it.

Still in the car, she continues the conversation with Gabriel inside her head. The scene is the same as fifteen minutes ago, in her front yard. He has no beard and looks much younger, about twenty, the age they met. She says, "Why are you here?" with a voice that's not her own. It's his voice. It has that quality of neediness that he developed after Anne's suicide.

Just then, she remembers the day Anne died. It was a Saturday morning, sunny but cold, a typical January weekend in Ottawa. It had snowed at least half a metre, and it took Gabriel over an hour and a half to shovel the driveway. She remembers his bright yellow winter jacket and black hat, the one she had bought for him in Mont-Tremblant, where the family used to go skiing for Christmas break every year.

Anne didn't eat much for breakfast that morning. Judith prepared crêpes just for her, with fresh strawberries, Nutella and maple syrup. But none of the sweets that were meant to appeal to her worked. She had lost her appetite, and there was little her parents could do about it. They weren't in the habit of forcing their child to do anything.

They had planned to spend the day cross-country skiing in Gatineau Park, but when Anne said no, they suggested spending the day at the National Art Gallery. Judith knew Anne loved experimental art; they'd brought their daughter to almost every exhibition at the Gallery, had even become members because of the girl's insatiable thirst. On more than one occasion, Gabriel had joked that Anne was a born artist, pride beaming in his green eyes.

Gabriel tried to entice Anne by telling her Janet Cardiff's *Forty-Part Motet* was on exhibition. "A sound sculpture," he said, and Judith, hopeful and helpless at the same time, repeated the same words, as if it would make a difference. Anne said she was tired and would read until their return.

The couple, oblivious, kissed their daughter goodbye and left for Gatineau Park with their skis and poles. Judith wore her dark blue outfit, matching ski pants and jacket. She never wore a hat, just earmuffs.

On their way, they spontaneously decided to stop in a small tourist village, Chelsea, to drink hot chocolate. She remembers Gabriel's hand on her thigh as they sat and talked, making plans for the summer. They thought that leaving the country might do Anne some good, and toyed between going to the south of Spain or else Latin America, since Anne had learned some Spanish in school. They decided to ask Anne what would be more interesting for her.

The trail was good, considering it had snowed so much the night before. The temperature was also very good, hovering at around −10°C. At one point, however, Judith fell over after feeling suddenly dizzy. She had a bad gut feeling and felt the need to call Anne. Gabriel dissuaded her, arguing that maybe their daughter needed some time alone. After all, she had received so much negative attention, and with the psychiatrist appointments, the police, and everything else, they didn't need to add to it. Judith let herself be convinced, and though her maternal instincts told her otherwise, she accepted the idea that Anne needed space.

When they got home, feeling recharged from the workout and fresh air, Gabriel was whistling Frank Sinatra's "Ol' Man River," Judith's favourite. He went straight to the bathroom, while Judith grabbed their ski gear to take it to the laundry room on the main floor of the house. There was so much to carry she had to do two runs. She called for Anne while she placed all the clothes on the drying rack and removed the liners from their boots, leaving them to dry as well. Then, she went to fetch a glass of water for herself. Gabriel met her in the kitchen, opened the fridge and asked her what they would have for lunch. It was already 2 p.m., Anne must be hungry.

They called and called for her, until Judith told him to go check on their daughter in her bedroom. She probably had her headphones on or had fallen asleep and couldn't hear them. When he came back down, shoulders raised, her heart skipped a beat. The bad feeling she had had earlier that day came back, more powerfully this time.

"I told you I should have called her," she said to him.

"Take it easy," he responded. "She's probably out with a friend."

What friend? What had he been thinking about? She shouldn't have listened to him when they were skiing. She should have called Anne.

They went their separate ways, her upstairs and him downstairs. When they met again, she was on her way down the stairs and he was waiting for her, his face pale and his mouth open.

"What? What? Where is she?"

He stopped her just as she was about to pass him. He held her arms with his large palms, and they faced each other silently for a few seconds. The expression on his face, his trembling lower lip and the look of horror in his eyes, scared her.

She began to sob, not knowing why. His eyes were red, on the verge of crying too.

"Where is she?" she demanded, this time louder. She tried to walk around him, but he held her back. She punched his arm, but he only held her tighter. His back hunched over and he hugged her, his body shaking as he silently cried.

She doesn't remember what happened next, doesn't know how she made it to the basement. She remembers only the strong light coming in from the windows, blinding her. Her daughter's body hung above the hardwood floor, which was wet with urine. Excrement dripped off her swollen feet onto the floor. She was wearing a pink sweater and black jeans. Her long black hair was up in a ponytail. Her face had turned blue. Dry blood lines, like snakes, wormed from her eyes, which had popped out of their sockets. Her neck bone was sticking out. It had broken after she had kicked the stool that lay sideways on the floor. The sight of her daughter like that was terrifying. Her baby's body was disgusting and broken. Judith tried to scream, but no sound escaped her.

The next thing she remembers is waking up in Gabriel's arms with paramedics and policemen talking and walking around her house. The next time she saw her daughter's body was at the hospital, after the autopsy. The doctor, an old man with a British accent, suggested the rope had been too short and that her death, which had taken "only about a minute," must have been gruesome and painful.

At this point, the memory mutates into a fantasy. Judith sees herself with a knife in one hand and her daughter's suicide note in the other, entering a small room made of stainless steel. No windows: only a single light bulb above the door. Four boys with demonic faces hang off the ceiling, their feet strapped in metal chains and their hands tied back. This recurring fantasy appeals to Judith's minimalist gothic tastes. The boys are naked, crying and jolting about. White cloths are tightly wrapped around their mouths, so that they can only grunt but not scream or talk. She imagines slitting their throats one by one and watching dark blood pour on the ground, just as her Anne's urine and excrement dripped on their home's hardwood floor four years ago. But just as she's about to slit the throat of the last boy, the fantasy mutates again, and she remembers the day Anne was born, remembers counting her baby toes, tears of happiness and exhaustion flowing down her cheeks. This unexpected happy memory, combined with the fantasy of murder, disturbs her.

She lets go of the wheel. Then she remembers she is in the car.

She sighs slowly. *Coreopsis*! The Latin name of the tickseed is *Coreopsis*.

# Four

When she pulls into the driveway of her architecture firm, a two-storey cube house, a young man sits on the doorstep, cigarette in hand. His beige suit is at least two sizes too big for him, she can tell from the car. The facade of the Platinum LEED-Certified house is made of dark wood planks that contrast with the metal door and enormous ten-by-ten windows through which you can see the entire décor of the office. The solar roof was Shannon's idea, as was the geothermal heating. Specializing in sustainable energy and green building was Shannon's idea, a way of differentiating Judith's work. Shannon, who is a talented businessperson and not an architect, is like a sister to her. And while she networked, landed contracts and managed the business, Judith was free to pitch ideas and create.

Judith sits in the car, buckled in and unmoving. She looks through the window, past the young man, and enters a space inside of her that is also somehow outside of her, right in her field of vision. Her mind seems to sail with the outside wind. When she notices this drifting, she becomes suddenly afraid of losing control. Control of what? She doesn't know.

She closes her eyes and breathes slowly. Look. The clouds are parting. What does the sky see? she wonders. What a terrifying sight it must be, to look down on earth.

The young man puffs out smoke. He wears small glasses made of dark metal. Maybe they're meant to age him, but they have the opposite effect. He looks like an adolescent. He is the intern, which means he's either in third year or has already finished his university degree. He flicks the cigarette to the ground and puts it out. His shoes are black and shiny. *Shiny black shoes.* This makes her laugh.

He stands up and straightens his suit jacket as Judith walks toward him. He extends his hand, smiling, waiting until she is close enough to shake it, close enough for him to say hello, cough, and say it again, this time with a more masculine voice. Something about his tone reminds her of Gabriel. They shake hands. His grip is weak, hers firm.

"I'm Cal," he says, cheeks turning pink.

She hasn't seen a man blush since, well, she can't remember since when. It's nice. She forces a smile back, thinking it might reassure him.

"Good," she responds.

The impulse to be polite, to welcome him, the whole ritual of first-day-at-work swiftly irritates her. She knows what it entails but she refuses to show him around the office, the back rooms and the storage upstairs. She doesn't want to be the one to decide where he should sit and work, or create an email account for him. The idea of showing him their portfolio, their client lists or even the kinds of materials they work with dampens her mood. Is that what's irritating her, or is the feeling merely coming out now, misplaced and delayed? Only in retrospect does she realize the impact of her encounter.

*You try not to think about Gabriel and his voice, but it's stronger than you, and while you know time has passed and you're now in front of someone else, you still feel the rush of energy that can only be discharged into your body by his voice – Gabriel's voice.*

"Looks like it's going to rain," he says.

"Yes, the clouds. But they're parting a little," she observes. Between the moment she says "yes" and the time it takes to arrive at the final "little," her thoughts have already trailed off to another place.

He rubs his nose and coughs again.

"Excuse me."

"What for?" she asks, somewhat annoyed.

She looks at him. Really looks at him. His face is round, with potential for passion and professionalism. Passion is physical before it's mental. It's in the strength and tension of the body. Cal's neck is tense, and so is his jaw. His eyes and mouth are relaxed, and his round glasses are slick. He signals with his suit and tie someone who is learned, even if he misses the mark somewhat. That is what she looks for in an intern: someone who is competent and spirited. Why is it so hard for Shannon to find someone with these two fundamental qualities?

Cal must be over six feet tall, as tall as Gabriel. Maybe taller. She's a mere five foot three. But she does not feel vulnerable in front of Cal. He's thin, verging on scrawny. The metal glasses, though small, are big for his face, just like his ears. He has short blond hair, cut military style. Something about his blue eyes, the way they stare at her with apparent emptiness, disturbs her. He feels familiar even though she is sure she has never seen him before. She finds him attractive in an ugly kind of way and suddenly feels repulsed.

"Wait here," she commands. "I have to grab my laptop and then we're off." Then she adds in Shannon's voice, "We have to leave, *like, fifteen minutes ago*." Interesting, she thinks, how we pick up other people's language, even their tone.

She pauses and considers the young man's blank look. Becomes aware of the fact that she has already forgotten his name.

"It's nice to meet you," she says and knows only the moment she has finished saying it that it's a lie. But why shouldn't it be nice to meet him? She regrets her feeling. Since how petty. Since she has yet to get to know him. In a kinder, more maternal voice, she adds, "Wait for me here, I'll go tell Shannon we're off."

She turns her back to him and walks toward the door, automatically searching for the BlackBerry in her purse.

"Yes. Thank you," he says, voice drifting.

His suit billows, subtly pushed by the wind. She slams the door behind her, feeling impatient and still troubled from her run-in with Gabriel.

Even on a cloudy day, the light enters with force into the open-concept design that is their office. There is a large wooden table with six chairs in the centre, where Shannon sits. A sofa and a small coffee table by the window. The table is bright green, the colour of their brand. Just to the left of the entrance is a long green shelf with models of museums, buildings and houses Judith has created. Hanging on the wall are posters with information about LEED certification and green architecture. It's all branded and very fancy. Certain words are repeated for effect: "sustainable architecture," "green design," "minimize negative environmental impact," and the line, "efficiency and moderation in the use of materials, energy and development space."

Everything is a mess inside the office – papers and textile samples and cardboard boxes scattered on every inch of the two tables – and the entire room seems to have left a trail of things pointing in the direction of Shannon, who is speaking on the phone. The word "perception" enters Judith's consciousness. It appears to be busy in here. Business is happening here.

Shannon acknowledges her entry with an enormous smile. Just looking at Shannon's straight white teeth and the enthusiasm that radiates from her face makes Judith feel heavy. She feels broken – no, in the process of breaking still.

Judith sinks into the sofa, her body moulding to its shape. As if forgetting how to sit, she half lies. Outside the window, Cal has lit another cigarette. His back to her, she cannot seem to reconstitute the details of his face in her mind. It requires too much imagination. She is too tired to form a thought about this.

Her fingers, with a will of their own, as if hands had their own centres of intelligence, take the BlackBerry out of its cover and open Instagram. Thumb scrolls down until she reaches @andandor's feed. It takes her a few seconds to realize what she sees.

The drawings are black and white; at the bottom are a play button and a time recording, as if of a YouTube video. The woman with Asian features, her hair up in a bun, is in a seated position while someone cuts a piece of her clothing with a pair of scissors. Her face is blank, with absolutely no sign of emotion. There are four drawings in total: two of people cutting her clothes, their bodies visible; the third is a close-up of the scissors and the hands that hold the object that cuts her shirt. The fourth is of the woman's legs and torso, with the pair of scissors beside her. The weapon is merely an object that, when at rest, lies docile on the floor.

Judith puts a hand against the window but doesn't notice she's there until she takes her eyes off the phone. Outside, Cal sits on the stairs, waiting for her. Who, if not her, stood up from the couch and walked over to the window? Yet she doesn't remember doing any of it. It was all automatic. Her mind was focused on the Instagram photos, which fascinate and disturb her at the same time.

"Judy!"

Shannon's smile is as intense as her tone of voice. When Judith smiles like that, with her mouth curved into a half moon, the muscles in her cheeks feel contrived.

"Why is Cal still outside?" asks Shannon.

Cal, thinks Judith, that's his name. She must find a way to remember it. Cal, like calendar. Her Calendar app, which is filled on a daily basis by Shannon and neglected just as fiercely by Judith. There is enough tension around that calendar for her to associate it with Cal's name.

"Is he sleeping? Poor boy. Have you met him already?" Shannon doesn't wait for a reply. She looks at her watch and her eyes open wide. "Oh my God, I'm so late. You're late too. You have to take him. I'm sorry, I know, I know. But I can't have him with me, and plus, they'll love him in Montréal. Young people bring life to projects, you know. Their marketing manager is only twenty-three. Can you believe it? Twenty-three, for God's sake."

"How old is the Calendar boy?"

"Who?" Shannon shakes her head. "You've already got a nickname for him, how romantic. I hope this one works out." The last sentence is not a statement. It's a whine, a request.

Judith sighs. She thinks about the pair of scissors in those photos. What could they possibly represent? Why did he post these images? They are completely different from his usual work. He usually makes portraits with spray paint on asphalt or building facades.

"Be good to him," says Shannon, tapping on Judith's shoulder, making a joke out of scolding her. This is their third intern in the past month; the first two were what Shannon called "total disasters." The first quit after a week and the second was let go of on the premise of "personality incompatibilities." Judith hated how much the young woman talked and how little she worked. On more than one occasion, Judith had caught her clicking likes on Facebook instead of working. That, plus the intern's habit of slurping at lunch time, was simply unbearable.

Shannon walks around the large wooden table and unfolds the adjustable trolley that's beside it. She says, "You'll love him. He won't bother you too much like the last one." That statement is an apology. Shannon places the mini house models into cardboard boxes and stacks them one by one on the trolley. "He's maybe a bit too quiet. But by your standards, I'm sure you won't notice." A nervous, unexpected laugh escapes her.

They hug and Shannon leaves. Outside, Cal helps her carry the trolley over the stairs. It strikes Judith that ramps aren't just for wheelchairs. Should they make their entrance more accessible? When Cal enters the office, she's sitting at the large wooden table, writing. First, his name. "C-A-L" in capital letters. Then the words: "Intern. Be nice to him." Finally, she writes a note to remind herself to make their office more accessible by adding a ramp. "Costs?" This question is for Shannon. "Benefits: access to wheelchairs and trolleys." This observation is for herself.

Cal smells like nicotine and something else. Sugar. She looks up at him from the corner of her eye. She is done writing but finds other words to put on the page. His mouth moves in circles like a washing machine. She concludes he's chewing gum, and, satisfied with her note, she puts down her pen.

"Is there a bathroom? Please?"

She points to the staircase. "Up. To your left."

"Thank you."

He nods with his forehead and nose. The soles of his shoes click loudly on the hardwood. There's something strange about Cal. He is at odds with his age. The other two interns were more like Shannon, outgoing and interested, even if, unlike her business partner, they turned out to be incompetent and somewhat arrogant. What is it about Cal? It's not just the suit. It's his way of being, stoic and stiff. His body language appears to be neutral, but she feels he's holding something back.

The moment he leaves her field of vision, she opens Instagram again. Who is this beautiful Asian woman and why is she letting them cut her clothes like that? Judith looks for clues. #YokoOno #cutpiece #performanceart #picturespictures. She opens Chrome and searches for "Yoko Ono Cut Piece." She finds the ten-minute YouTube video of the 1960s performance filmed by Albert and David Maysles.

The action is immediate. Yoko Ono sits on stage. She's young, beautiful and passive. *Is she actually passive or are you merely interpreting her body language as such? The artist created the performance piece, and she is therefore probably in control of its parameters, is she not?* But as a black-haired woman cuts a piece of Ono's cardigan, Judith realizes that no one is in control of the audience. They are participating. They are spontaneous. Yoko Ono's body is completely vulnerable.

Above, the toilet flushes. She presses fast-forward as the sound of the running water stops. Snap: the bra strap has been cut by a man. Nervous laughter from the audience. The camera is hand-held. Shaky. A chill runs down Judith's spine.

Ono crosses her arms and holds her bra from falling, her face motionless. She shows no emotions. So she *is* in control: of herself and her reaction to the scene.

Cal is in front of her, waiting. Lips tight, eyes serious, she puts her phone back in her purse.

"Grab that box," she says. "We're running late."

Judith drives quietly, at the speed limit and with the radio off.

She thinks she should say some words.

What year is he in? He has graduated. *But he looks so young.* How old is he? Twenty-two. Will he get his master's in architecture? No. No, what? He doesn't want to be an architect. His degree is in environmental sciences.

Getting him to speak is like pulling teeth. No, that idiom isn't right. It's like hunting deer, you have to be persistent, patient, and beyond that, you have to like hunting. Talking for the sake of talking deeply annoys Judith.

There is no traffic on Highway 417 East. They've passed the city's invisible border. Rows of trees frame the road. Hard to tell what kind of birds fly above the forest, roaming. The blackbirds that cross the road to and fro captivate her. The mood, traced in their shadows, resembles her. It's as if they're chasing each other. One of them pushes the other with its feet. She cannot tell if they are playing or fighting and she finds the scene strangely moving. As if she isn't part of it, as if she's observing it from the outside in.

Look. The young man, Calendar, Cal, is biting his nails. He probably needs a cigarette. He's looking out the window, at the birds, at the chaotic clouds, at God-knows-what.

"If you studied environmental sciences, why are you doing an internship with an architecture firm?" And she wonders, in her own head, why Shannon approved him.

Yes, that is the question she wants to ask him. Or maybe not. She wants to know who he is. Not who he is, necessarily, but what pressures have moulded him. Yes, that's what she wants to know, but she isn't sure how to formulate the question.

He says he studied environmental sciences because, well (he rubs his chin), it seemed better than engineering and not as hard.

"Of course," he says, trying to compensate by lowering his tone and looking more serious, "I think we need to build more sustainable structures that respond to global pressures on our natural resources and the environment in general. My undergraduate thesis was on new technologies and green architecture in residential and commercial buildings."

He wipes his palms on his pants. He's nervous, then? The cigarettes, the nail biting – maybe it could all be traced back to an extreme case of insecurity? Could she remember being young and starting out?

She started her own firm after Anne was born. Gabriel stayed at home, and she went to work when the baby was only one. In retrospect (*always in retrospect*), she regrets the decision. She wishes she had stayed at home with her daughter. Wishes, wishes.

The wind is against them. She can feel it in her hands, as she grips the wheel, and in her foot, the one that's on the accelerator. The car, which she has been driving for five years, is like an extension of her. She can sense everything about it.

*Admit you are uneasy around Cal. You think he's strange because you cannot perceive him in any way that fits easily within a predetermined category. He is young but acts old. He appears calm, his face gives no signal of alarm, and yet his body is nervous.*

"What do you know about architecture?"

He shifts in his seat. "Not much. I mean, I know a lot of theory, but this is my first professional experience."

"Tell me what you know."

He pauses. "When I was young, I spent a lot of time on my grandparents' property just outside Ottawa. They had a hobby farm, with sheep, cows, pigs, chickens and bees."

What the hell is he talking about? wonders Judith.

Unaware of his employer's expectations, Cal goes on. "I loved beehives, not the ones my grandpa made, but the ones you find in nature. They're beautiful. I could spend days looking for them, like a pirate looking for treasure. And when I found one, I'd photograph it in earnest. Bees are architects, in a way." He stops to look at her, but she doesn't acknowledge his gaze. "I probably still have those photos laying around somewhere. My thesis project focused on architecture that echoes natural landscapes and uses sustainable materials."

"Can you tell me what you know about resource-efficient building life cycles?" she asks.

He parrots the words "life cycles."

Is she driving an intellectually challenged young man to Montréal?

"Do you know what LEED certification is?"

"It's what you specialize in, right?"

She hates it when a person answers a question with a question. Someone grave and scornful comes out of a deep sleep within her – a woman that she repressed a long time ago. The moment she recognizes this, she raises her head and looks in the rear-view mirror. Her unsmiling face frightens her. She remembers that when she first started her business, she was confused and terrified. She almost lost her first client because she felt intimidated by the old man. He was a dentist and wanted to demolish a residential house and turn it into a commercial office. She remembers his black moustache and large aviator glasses. His nose hair needed a trim. When she mispronounced his name for the third time, something Polish, which she should have been able to pronounce considering she was Eastern European (or so he had told her), he shook his head and belittled her. What he said exactly, she can't remember. But from that moment onward, she was always nervous in his presence, and it was the least pleasant of all her jobs. She never asked for a recommendation from him and for many years afterward avoided clients whose names she might mispronounce.

"You'll learn as you go," she says, matter-of-fact. She meant her voice to sound friendly, but it comes out in a foreign tone, strict and condescending.

The thing she wants to find out about him, who he is, suddenly seems impossible to grasp.

He says, "Why did you become an architect?"

She laughs. She liked to build things, she says, ever since she was young. She played with blocks and then later, with Legos, and was naturally fascinated by the processes of creation and destruction. When she finishes speaking, the words she has uttered surprise her. Of course, she knows she likes to build things, but she has never said it like that, with the words "creation" and "destruction" side by side.

"I liked Legos too," he says.

The atmosphere in the car changes. It's lighter, more amicable. Then she attempts to make a joke, something about a Lego castle and a clumsy little girl that simply could not build a round structure, and then feels absurd and trivial, and stops. The mood, like an elastic, has been stretched one too many times in directions she could not control. She needs peace now.

Cal, unable to read her mind, continues to talk. He says he applied to her firm because his father, who is a green engineer, knows Shannon. *So it was nepotism. You're not surprised. There is simply no way he could have passed a regular interview.*

"Who is your father?"

"Greg Morales."

The name means nothing to her.

Silence once again enters the car. They pass families of elm trees with pale green foliage. Behind them stands a troupe of towering pine trees.

Her face folds with curiosity as she remembers Yoko Ono's black-and-white body. The images by @andandor and the YouTube video mould into one. She recreates the ghostly, eerie scene of the man that snaps off Yoko Ono's bra and comments over it, as if she were writing the voice-over of a documentary, "She sits, legs folded, face blank, eyes void of emotion, as the man clutches the metal instrument that could kill her, but does not. He cuts the straps of her bra and they fall but do not completely expose her. She holds her breasts with her hands crossed, making an 'X', as if spelling out a limit, an inarticulable 'no.'"

A poisonous sensation runs down her spine as she fully realizes the meaning of Cal's last name. She turns and looks at him, fingers in his mouth like a baby, chewing the tips of his nails.

"What's your name?" she asks.

"Cal."

"No," she says in a deadly tone. "Your full name."

"Calvin Morales."

An inarticulable 'no'.

At first there is nothing, a space empty or filled with void, whatever you want to call it. Something heavy and uncomfortable settles in her chest, just below the neck, like a brick. It makes breathing difficult.

His name is Calvin Morales.

*Calendar Cal is Calvin Morales.*

She doesn't interpret his name in the expected, routine way. It blows her mind. She loses the sense of touch in her hands. As if her body is going numb, she knows she is steering the wheel but cannot actually feel it.

*Oh my God. What are you going to do?*

"Are you okay?" he asks in a slow and uneasy way.

The stormy sky, with its greyness, enters her skull. Confusion masks the anger and fear that brew inside her at an astonishing rate.

The brick moves up, to her throat, and settles on the back of her tongue, threatening to asphyxiate her.

They pass an Esso gas station. She signals her intention to turn right, but the next exit isn't for another two kilometres.

Automatically, her hands guide the wheel in a clockwise direction. When she hears a horn blare, she jumps and quickly steers back into her lane. This is the first time in a long time she has forgotten to check before turning. The car passes her. She avoids the driver's glare. She is so frightened that her tremulous hands do not attempt to change lanes again. They stay moulded to the wheel for another five minutes, until there is an exit. She and the boy sit in unbreakable and unbearable silence, both afraid and confused, but for vastly different reasons.

# Five

*When you put the car in park, you have no idea you're about to turn the engine off, slam the door and lead him into Ottawa's greenbelt forest. You have no idea you're about to ask him if he knows your full name, all of it, especially your last name. In other words: if he knows who you are in relation to him. The sky is trembling with discontent and you hear thunder. You should be driving straight to Montréal. Stopping now will not only make you late, it guarantees your absence at the meeting.*

"No," he says. He doesn't know her last name.

That's what she thought.

"What high school did you go to?"

"Immaculata."

With that word, he confirms her suspicion. The brick descends to her stomach.

She takes the key out, fingers trembling. She unbuckles and reaches for her purse in the back. She throws the keys in, and the jingling stops.

"Are you okay?" he asks. He looks worried. Maternal, even, if that's the right word.

She says she needs air. She exits the car and slams the door. The humidity in the air is heavy. There is no doubt it will rain today. It's cold, and the wind lifts her hair. The thick hair, the same her daughter had, makes a black curtain over her eyes.

He is gentle with the car door. She hears the sound of paper, then a few soft click-click-clicks – lighter and fire. He's smoking, exhaling deeply.

She turns to face him. His eyes still wear that worried look, *as they should*. The way he stands, with his feet shoulder-width apart, knees bent, back foot at an angle and front foot pointing toward her – his position reminds Judith of the fencing bouts she's seen at the RA Centre, a few rooms away from her shooting range. She shakes her head as if trying to rattle away the thoughts.

"What year did you graduate?" she asks.

"2012."

"A year late?"

"Yes, how did you know?"

She swings her hand, as if waving away a mosquito.

"What held you back?" she asks. She tightens her belt around her waist. Her purse is squeezed tight under her left arm.

He looks away, takes a drag of his cigarette, and then settles his gaze on the clouds that hover low in the sky. "Personal stuff."

She scoffs. *Personal stuff.*

"Are you okay to drive?" he asks, before drawing deeply again from the cigarette.

"No." She's not okay to drive. No: she's not okay.

"Want to go for a walk?" he asks, as if he were a man of forty. "When I was little," he adds, "my grandpa and I used to go to the forest, and he'd identify the fauna and flora for me." She is surprised by this comment. *What on earth is he talking about?*

He says, "It used to relax me. Cheer me up, you know?" Holding the cigarette between his fingers, he points toward the small path that leads into the dark green forest and its black shadows. She follows him, breathing heavily, taking small steps.

He points to the trees and gives their Latin names, followed by anecdotal and interesting facts, or a small note, brief and transcendental like a haiku, on their beauty. She can tell that he paid attention in his environmental sciences classes, but she has a hard time focusing on what he says. The hackberry, for example, also known as the *Celtis occidentalis*. Well, did she know that its leaves look like hearts? Or that it was previously considered part of the elm family or the *Celtidaceae* family, but the new classification system placed *Celtis* in the hemp family? He laughs nervously, cigarette still in his mouth. Hemp. Hemp, as in cannabis.

She barely listens to him. She feels disoriented: *who is Cal*? She wants to stabilize him, crystallize him, into one exact sentence that her mind can accept as concrete. He is her nervous intern, in need of serious training. He is a smart young man who loves nature, much like her. He is one of the four boys ...

Judith remembers the Facebook posts that haunted Anne, that gave others permission to humiliate her, and that prompted her to drop out of high school and fall into an abyss of pain. The hum of Judith's laptop as she saw, for the first time, the blurry photograph of her daughter kneeling in front of a black-haired boy, his hand on her ponytail. His pants were down on the floor. She remembers the fucking look of pride on his drunken face. The collision between sight and sound, memory collapsing several sensations into one fragmented impression: "whore," "nerd on sperm," "rich bitch down on her knees," et cetera, these and other comments on Facebook, hateful language that had contaminated Judith and rendered her sick with anger, disgust and fear. She remembers the night she discovered Anne was cutting her inner thighs; the ride over to the hospital where doctors and patients would soon know their faces, their names and their personal story from TV and newspapers.

Now, with each step that leads her deeper into the forest, her nausea grows. The veins in her neck pulsate to an atavistic rhythm. No doubt adrenalin is rushing through her entire system, preparing her body for the duel to come. She wonders if Cal took that photo or if he's one of the two boys who watched – perverted accomplices to her daughter's degradation. She tries to remember Cal's face from the seven photographs the RCMP shared with her and Gabriel. Fragments, broken links, the incompleteness of the past, rising to surface again. She can't remember. She sees in the back of her mind the image of her daughter's limp body, hanging from the basement ceiling. A voice inside her wants to scream.

He stops, turns and looks at her. Says the tree in front of them produces stone fruit, also known as drupe, which sustains many species. It's dry and sweet, reminiscent of a date.

She nods, though she hasn't heard a word of what he's said. She watches him, distracted and anxious, while a perplexing paleness sucks the colour out of her face.

"Are you alright ma'am?" He takes a last puff and meticulously rubs the tip of the cigarette, letting the ash fall. Then, he takes out his pack, a grey Benson & Hedges to fit the mood of the day, and leaves his bud inside. As he does this, his eyes never lose sight of her. Judith senses his gaze, the way it assesses and appraises her, and she feels two sharp pangs, like needles, pierce her heart plexus.

*You think he's responsible – caring for the environment with small gestures that speak volumes, and it makes you shake your head in disbelief. Why is he calling you "ma'am" all of a sudden? Can he sense what is to come? And why the concern in his eyes? You don't believe what you see. Your muscles flex. You want to scream. Want to grab and throw his body over the forest, watch it from an eagle's eye as it flies over the waistline of Ottawa's greenbelt and lands somewhere in the middle of the highway. Splash. No more Cal. No more pain. No more, no more.*

Her vision disturbs her and she takes a step back, horrified.

He moves toward her, as if to provide her with some kind of support, but she stops him by raising her hand.

"Let's keep moving," she says.

He nods and, like a good boy, leads the way deeper into the forest. Above, the sky is a patchwork of dark grey spots, visible between branches of green foliage. The wind blows hard, rattling the leaves.

A chipmunk crosses their path and Cal doesn't miss the opportunity to speak in his wavering voice, which attempts to sound entertaining but fails. He fumbles and his confidence sounds false and hollow. Who is this perfect stranger? she wonders again. If only she had a specific memory of this boy – when he was in grade nine or ten or eleven. But how could she? She never made it to any of the school activities. School functions were Gabriel's job.

"The chipmunk, spelled m-u-n-k, not m-o-n-k, a common mistake, is a rodent from the *Sciuridae* family. They're quite specifically North American, with the sole exception of the Siberian chipmunk, which lives in Asia." Did she know that their genus name, "*Tamias*," was Greek for "treasurer" or "housekeeper?"

She does not answer. She stops following him.

Unaware that she's watching him from behind, he continues.

"*Tamias* refers to their role in plant dispersal through their habit of collecting and storing food for winter." Then, he raises his finger in the air and, with an enthusiastic voice, a voice that's obviously reached its peak of elegance, filled with passion and ease, he claims, excited and eager, like a child, that she will not believe the serendipitous coincidence between the chipmunk and Ottawa. He looks at her with beaming eyes and, since she is non-responsive, declares, "Did you know the common name may have originally been 'chitmunk' from the Odawa word '*jidmoonh*', meaning 'red squirrel'?" Then, he chuckles, following the rodent with his gaze, and adds, "I know Ottawa and Odawa aren't the same, but phonetically they're pretty close, plus, I'm pretty sure the Odawa have a reserve near Ottawa in the States."

He stops and turns, grinning proudly and exposing his yellowed teeth.

When he sees her standing on a small rock, holding the pistol in her hands, his face drops, his smile disappears and his eyes widen.

"Come closer," she says, her voice trembling.

He remains immobile.

"Lift your hands."

He doesn't respond other than to turn his head sideways, as if looking for something.

"Do you know who I am?" she asks.

He raises his hands in the air. She knows if she were standing close to him, he'd be twice her height with his hands up like that. But the distance between them and the rock below her feet give her the impression of being taller and bigger – a stronger opponent.

"My name is Judith Belović."

Nothing.

"Judith Belović," she repeats. She closes an eye and aims at him with the SW1911. Its slick side is like a straight line connecting her directly to her past. She aligns the pistol's rear and front sights to aim directly at Cal's head. His eyes, she can see, are filled with terror. So he recognizes her. *Good.*

"Move," she says, tilting her head quickly to the left.

His Adam's apple bobs as he swallows hard. He turns to go and is interrupted by her voice. "Slowly." In his oversized suit, he slowly steps off the path and enters the forest, the wind moving with him, pushing him along.

They are somewhere in the greenbelt, ten to fifteen minutes away from the small parking lot where her car sits, but it feels as if they are a lifetime away from people, all regular life. All around them are tall pines. The citrusy smell reminds her of weekends spent hiking in Gatineau Park with Anne and Gabriel. She remembers Gabriel wearing green shorts. She had always found his muscular legs quite attractive. She remembers this one time when Anne needed to pee but refused to do it in the bushes. Finally, after fifteen minutes of holding it and the nearest washroom being another half-hour hike, she did it. Gabriel and Judith could not resist giggling when Anne came back, face red, eyes near tears because a mosquito had bit her in the ass.

They stand two metres apart, if that, facing each other.

His suit jacket, dress shirt, pants and shoes are beside him. He stands shaking, skin covered in goosebumps, in his brown socks and boxers. When she asked him to get undressed, he'd made no resistance, no opposition, not a hint of rivalry.

Dark blue with a hockey stick and puck pattern – her focus is shaken by Cal's flashy boxers. They remind her he is young and she doubts her purpose for a millisecond. He's so thin. His collarbones and rib cage stick out as though he were malnourished. His armpit hair and the few hairs below his belly button are blondish and light brown, and barely visible.

His boyish body reminds her of his possible innocence. Worse, it evokes the mother in her. Something in her is worried about him, and she hears a voice inside her asking him to get dressed before he catches a cold. To suppress the unwelcome voice, she tests him.

"You're one of the four boys, right?"

Silence. His hands begin a slow descent toward his waist.

"Up!" she yells and up they jolt.

"Speak!" Her voice frightens her. Her thighs tremble slightly, and she flexes her muscles in order to keep her legs anchored to the ground.

He begins to cry. Tears flow down his long bony nose, resting at the back of his nostrils before flooding his mouth, chin, and finally dropping to the ground.

A burning sensation ripples across her chest, like hot oil being poured over her breasts, burning her muscles and lungs. "Speak," she says slowly, pronouncing the word with emphasis. "Speak. Or I will kill you."

His shaking grows so violent that he stumbles and then regains his balance. He evidently did not anticipate this attack and is in a state of shock, and the tears, the runny nose and the moss of spit around the corners of his lips turn his serious, mature face into that of a child or perhaps even a helpless toddler or an infant. He wheezes, stops, shakes and continues to wheeze. His long arms wobble and his knees tremble. He looks as though he's about to drop.

She tightens her grip around the SW1911, which she holds with both hands. She lowers her body carefully, keeping her aim and gaze directly on his face. With her free hand, she picks up the purse, which is on the ground beside her. Keeping her eyes on him, she places the bag over her shoulder and opens it. She takes out her BlackBerry and lets the purse drop. The smack it makes hitting the forest ground makes him shriek and his fear, so intense and genuine, touches her. She feels a flash of compassion but forces it down. *If you let the feeling linger, it may take over.*

Her eyes move quickly back and forth between his face and her BlackBerry. She unlocks it and her Instagram shows the image of Yoko Ono sitting beside a pair of scissors. Judith's shoulders relax. Her frown dissipates and her lips become a straight line. Yes, it's clear to her what the scissors represent now.

She looks at Cal and sees a vulnerable body, completely at her mercy. She knows she has already crossed the line, legally. She has committed a crime. She has already damaged him. Vengeance is hers. Why not stop now?

*No. One more thing.*

Her experienced thumb exits Instagram and flips through her apps until it finds the image of a microphone. She opens her Voice Recorder app and places the BlackBerry, very carefully, on top of her purse.

"Four and a half years ago," she says, her voice having lost some of its venom. "You and three other boys went into the basement of a house and took photos of my daughter." She stops. Her jaw muscles tighten. Without thinking, she flips off the safety on her pistol.

"Speak, or you die," she says in the most unrecognizable voice. A voice so deep, so ancient and so filled with rage that both of them breathe more rapidly. "What happened? Which one of them were you? The one who photographed, hmm?" She takes a small step toward him and his wheezing grows desperate.

"The one who pulled down his pants? Hmm? Did you force her to kneel down or did you drug her?"

His face is ghostly pale. His head shakes. She stands a metre away from him and the gun is only a few centimetres from his face.

"Sh-she-she wa-waa – she ... We – "

"What?"

His eyes open and close. It's as though he's coming in and out of consciousness.

"Drun-drunk. We were drunk."

"Did you or did you not get her drunk? Was she aware of what she was doing?"

"I d – I don't know."

It begins to rain. Big, heavy, loud raindrops. She is soaked in less than ten seconds, and his lips turn a shade darker. The mother in her is loud, louder than before. He's going to catch a cold, she wants to yell, and to protect herself from this voice she opens her jaw wide and exhales, as if letting some unwanted spirit escape her throat.

Her first instinct is to protect the BlackBerry. She places it in her pocket and grabs her purse. She must keep it working. She must make sure to record his confession. She will not stop until he has confessed fully, in as much incriminating detail as possible.

"Go," she says. "Move." But the pine tree doesn't offer the kind of protection she's looking for. The trunk is just tall enough for her to hide under the crown of the tree, but not tall enough for Cal. He hunches and leans on the trunk, but the rain, which is falling on an angle, hits them with the same intensity as before. She finds they are too close together under the same tree.

Leaving his clothes behind, they walk in search of another shelter, him in front of her.

*What happens to a gun when it gets wet? Does it stop working?*

He trips and falls. He rolls to the left, over a rock about the size of a basketball, and lands on his back. She has an unexpected flashback of Anne falling over in much the same way when she was about ten. She had tripped on a rock when they were vacationing in Newfoundland. Judith keeps her gun steady. His left leg is bleeding. He grunts and puts his hand on the wound, rocking his upper body back and forth. The sight of blood makes her sick, and she has to look away, breathe deeply. He sits on the forest floor and cries.

"I want my mother," he whimpers, and the words make a fist in her chest.

She lowers the gun a moment; she takes off her trench coat and throws it at him. He doesn't react and the coat lands on his head before sliding off, onto the forest floor.

"Put it on," she says. He doesn't move. "Put it *on*."

He tips over and slumps onto the ground. She can see that the wound is not deep but it hasn't stopped bleeding.

"Damn it!" she says. Holding the gun in her right hand, she kneels to the ground beside him. With her free hand, she attempts to wrap the coat around his leg, but it's impossible, and the whole time she's worried he'll kick her in the face. She tells him to help her remove the belt and, to her surprise, he does so without protest. She moves back and he wraps the coat himself, then takes the belt and secures his makeshift bandage as best he can.

She sits on the ground, legs crossed, about two metres away, a distance she considers safe for herself, just in case he attempts to attack her. Damn it, again. She forgot the BlackBerry in the pocket of her trench coat.

She stands and looks at him. His eyes are closed and he appears to be sleeping. Is he planning a trick? He looks so bleak and chilled, he might catch hypothermia.

"Open your eyes," she commands. She expects he will ignore her, but instead he opens his piercing blue eyes. They are cold, empty. The absence of feeling makes her wonder whether he's capitulating or planning retaliation. She anticipates all of Cal's potential counter-attacks in her mind, ready for anything.

The mark of a great fencer is always, without exception, her ability to control the opponent's confidence, to influence his sense of ability.

"Sit."

He sits, facing her. The left side of his face is covered in mud. It looks like a black stripe is painted on his right cheek from the corner of the eye to the jawline. The dark earth gives him the air of an aboriginal warrior, of the kind she has seen in countless Western films, or pop culture posters that feature men wearing war paint.

"In the pocket of my jacket is my phone. It's recording our conversation as we speak. It's in a waterproof case," she adds. *Why are you being so transparent with him right now? Think. Think before you speak.*

The sound of the rain is like a thousand mallet rolls hitting the drum of the forest floor. It is roaring. He looks demoralized, like a man on the edge of death. His furrowed brows sink deep, creasing his forehead. His lips have abandoned all expression; they are simply two flat lines above his chin, ready to accept whatever fate awaits them without resistance. Maybe all creatures have that look when they suspect they're about to die? Or maybe she's reading him wrong. She isn't sure if it's the fatigue, the unfriendly weather or something else that has locked his jaw so tightly.

"Were you one of the four boys that sexually assaulted my daughter, Anne Dumont-Belović?" Water streams down into her eyes. With her free hand, she moves her wet hair to the backs of her ears.

He lowers his eyes. Looks at his leg and examines the makeshift bandage. Or maybe not. Maybe he's looking at the BlackBerry in the pocket.

The rain starts to subside. Her vision becomes a little clearer. His lips are purple. His skin is white and muddy. She is amazed at how transformed he is from when she picked him up earlier that day. He looks as if he'd been stranded in the forest for a week, fighting for his life.

Behind his wet glasses, he looks at her with cold-blooded eyes. They seem to be daring her. A cold chill runs down her spine. She realizes she's shaking from a mixture of cold and fear. Her lips are probably as purple as his.

She knows she must keep him uncertain of her next move. She is hyperaware of the distance between them and intuitively shifts her footing so as to leap if and when need be.

"What happened that night when you took my daughter into the basement of Bob McLean's house? He was one of the four boys, wasn't he?"

He nods.

"Speak," she orders.

"Yes."

"What happened?" she demands.

"We were drunk."

"Did you slip something in her drink?"

His jaw flexes.

"We were all drunk." His Adam's apple moves slowly, as if he's swallowing something. His shoulders rise and fall with the rhythm of his breathing. "Everyone was drunk."

She nods. Then she stands and towers over him. She feels large, larger than life. From her perspective, the gun is bigger than his entire head.

"I'm going to kill you," she asserts, and the words dramatically alter her perception. She feels vast, like the entire greenbelt. Her power rests in her fingertips and she can claim a human life at any second. Vengeance is hers.

"You know this is sacred land?" he asks, his voice unsure. His shoulders are wobbly and he looks away from her.

"What?"

"Unceded and unsurrendered Algonquin territory."

"What are you talking about?" she asks, irritated.

"Well," he says, clearly stalling her. "This is not our land. This is the land of an ancient culture which values peace."

Judith frowns. She relaxes her stance, moved by Cal's pathetic attempt to save his life. She finds this moment ironic, filled with false hope and bitterness, and is conscious it may be a distraction, a maladapted feint.

He continues, "They had a way of life that involved peace and justice. You know, these were fundamental values then as now." He coughs and shivers violently. "There was always doorway after doorway to peace, and barrier after barrier to war."

A fierce and sore silence separates them.

"It was called 'The Way of The Heron,'" he explains, his voice filled with conviction and sudden strength of spirit. "Those who walked this way never engaged in violence, unless it was absolutely necessary. They considered violence a failure, you know. They had seven cycles of sevens which they followed – "

She interrupts him with a pointed and stinging "Shut the fuck up."

*What the fuck is wrong with this guy? Is he somehow mentally impaired? Can he not see, with his eyes, with his brain, with all of his five senses, that you're winning? That you're about to kill him?*

She takes one step forward. Two. Three.

He closes his eyes and begins to shudder again, and she feels an immense thrill. The power between her hands is incredible. She is aware of nothing except the feeling of absolute dominance. God is dead; she is God, creating her own meaning and values by cutting through the present moment with superhuman strength. She is law. She rules over Cal the way the sky rules over earth. She is the quintessential artist/tyrant, shaping her own destiny, fierce and ferocious. The moment she reaches the tip of her feverish feeling, it awakens another voice within her. *You've gone mad, Judith, you've finally realized your most violent fantasy and have become Machiavellian enough to enjoy the thrill of it.* Who is this voice inside of her? she wonders. Who are all of these voices and who are they speaking to? Perhaps she has reached the edge of consciousness and is in fact parachuting into madness.

The barrel is flat against his forehead. Touché, she thinks.

"Kneel," she says, and he does. He doesn't do it easily, because his leg must hurt, but he does as he's told. He favours the unhurt leg as he climbs into kneeling position.

"Were you the one who took the photos?"

His shaking is so severe that she has to remove the barrel from his forehead. Now, the sight of his distress amuses her. She senses something in her that finds all of this funny and surreal. She tells herself that if she's going to go to jail for this later, she might as well prolong his suffering. She thinks of her daughter, her dead body in the basement, and this intensifies her wish to torture Cal. To make him pay.

"I repeat: were you the one who posted the photos on Facebook?"

He crosses his arms across his chest, holding onto his shoulders, shaping an "X" across his torso.

She lowers herself to eye level. If he attempts to hit her, she can deflect his attack. The gun is millimetres away from his face. Seeing the weapon, he closes his eyes, expecting the end.

"Look at me," she whispers. She is disgusted by her own invitation, the way it sounds, as if she were speaking to Gabriel when they were intimate.

Again, this time louder: "Look at me."

The moment he looks at her, it's as if something inside of him breaks. He exhales deeply, lowering his head and shaking it left to right, like a pendulum.

"It wasn't me," he says. "It was Bobby. He did it. I was just at the wrong place at the wrong time, I swear." He repeats this sentence again as if attacking her with the only weapon at his disposal: words. He cries like a madman and the more desperate his outward lament, the angrier she gets. She realizes that nothing he says will satisfy her. Her gut feeling tells her he's lying, defending himself. No matter what he says, it will not bring back Anne.

Keeping the gun at the level of his face, she rises. Then she moves the gun toward his mouth. She forces his lips open with the tip of the barrel. His eyes open wide in surprise. A nasty moan escapes him. His breathing is heavy, the air moving with force through his nose. Tears mix with the rain and mud on his face. His nails jam into his collarbones as she forces the barrel further into his mouth. He attempts to scream – the muscles in his neck grow taut – but all that comes out is a muffled gargle.

*What are you going to do now? Kill him? Put him out of his misery?*

She looks at him intensely. She cannot see the answer to her questions in the scene in front of her. His mouth is full. The gun is loaded. Her fingers are ready. *What are you going to do?*

Her consciousness doesn't permit her to pull the trigger. It simply refuses to kill another human being, even if there are parts of her that want to punish him. It seems like the logical conclusion to the scenario she's orchestrated, and yet, she cannot pull the damn trigger. She feels split in two and does not know which side to associate herself with: the one that wants vengeance or the one that wants peace.

The long neck of the gun comes out of his mouth. He coughs, cries and spits.

"Kill me," he begs. "Kill me now."

*Why is he tempting you to attack?*

She isn't listening to Cal's invitation. She is somewhere inside of herself. It's impossible to tune out the voices that are judging her, telling her she's a monster. They ask how she could face Cal's mother. What would she say to her? She's done to him what they did to her Anne. Cal's sharp cry tortures her consciousness. Judith unconsciously puts the safety back on and slightly lowers the gun.

She does not see Cal's arm swing at her. She only feels the impact of his hard fist on her chest, and the shock is more startling than the physical pain. She falls to the ground, groaning, and is frightened because of the suddenness of his attack.

The gun drops out of her hand but she is quick – she scrambles after the weapon. It is wet, slippery, and almost slides through her fingers. But she has it – *thank you, God*. The initial feeling of fear is quickly followed by a bout of hatred for the boy. Humiliation shadows her surprise, and she feels an intensified desire for revenge. How dare he attack her, after she felt a moment of pity for him and his mother?

Cal is on all fours, facing the barrel once again. He looks like a mad dog. His eyes are red, set aflame. Her trench coat hangs off his leg like a stuck piece of toilet paper.

"You crazy bitch," he says. "What do you want?" There is real desperation in his voice. She finds him pathetic and yet is terrified by him.

"Take off your boxers," she commands.

"No."

She has to make a decision. He's stronger than her. He can kill her with his bare hands if he gets the chance.

"I don't have to kill you right now," she says calmly. "I can shoot you in the arm. Is that what you want?"

Something passes over his face, a feeling or a mood accompanied by a nervous twitch in his eyelids. It's not easy to interpret its meaning. Maybe a temporary loss of confidence, or the tip of a line of rage – who knows?

"I wasn't the one who took photos," he says, his lips barely moving.

She's interested.

"And I didn't do to her what you just did to me, you whore. You bitch. If you don't kill me now, I'll kill you."

"Careful what you wish for," she says in a solemn and emphatic manner. That voice. God, her voice has changed. She knows now without a doubt that she can kill him if she needs to.

He knows it too.

He retreats and makes himself comfortable by sitting cross-legged on the damp ground. Then, he extends his hurt leg and bends the healthy one.

"Speak," she declares, and he takes out the BlackBerry. Throws it at her. It lands on her stomach, winding her slightly.

"Ha!" She laughs at his futile act of violence. How little it changes, she thinks to herself. She has the gun. So long as she has the gun, she leads the dance.

The voice recorder is still running. 37 minutes and 23 seconds, 24 seconds, 25, 26 ...

Has it been that long? How quickly time passes. She sees two missed calls in the upper-left corner. The voicemail icon is up, too. She suddenly remembers her life. She remembers her name. Her job. Montréal.

The wave of regret, when it hits the shore of her consciousness, hits so hard it almost spills over into parts of her that feel defenceless.

# Six

*What have you done? Oh my God. You're going to go to jail. What were you thinking? You'll never get away. You're going to lose your job, your house, your reputation. Then, another voice. Much darker: the only way out is to end it. You have to kill him. Save yourself.*

He looks for signs on her face, she can tell by the way his eyes move, as if he were reading the lines of a book.

"You're going to kill me," he says point-blank. "You don't have a choice. Or you're fucked."

She nods.

The trees and grass, though green and brown, appear colourless. The grey sky seems to have seeped into everything, sucking nature of its life-force and luminosity.

"Then I'll tell you. Your daughter was a whore like you."

He is provoking her. She squints.

"No one liked her at school," he says. "She had no friends. She was a nerd. Weird. Jordan invited her to the party as a joke. It wasn't planned. She was easy. Practically salivated when Bobby unzipped his pants. Jordan, the quarterback – you know him? He's huge – took photos on his cellphone. What a moron. We didn't know he was doing that. What a pervert, that guy, I swear. What a loser, I hate him. Fuck him! It's because of him the police came after us. What an idea: to take photos and post them on Facebook as evidence. Can you believe that guy? Bobby hadn't done anything against Anne's will, you get that? My only crime was to have been in the same room when she and Bobby were getting it off. None of my business. Anyway, like I said, Steve and I were simply at the wrong place at the wrong time. We're not – never were – friends with Bobby and Jordan, they intimidate and bully everyone. They're the ones you're after."

She sits, frozen, but tears are streaming down her face. At the edge of her anger, she can sense a deep sorrow.

"What?" he says. "Did you think Bobby forced her?"

*Is he telling you the truth? There's no way to know.*

She lowers her gun and finds it difficult to breathe. Cal has wounded her, though not through any direct action. She is mentally destabilized and losing strength. Judith takes a step back, retreating.

Cal fingers the wet earth, in search of something. "I went back upstairs," he says. "I let the gang have their fun. I didn't think there was any foul play. She seemed to be enjoying her – "

"Enough!"

"Why?" he asks, his hand full of soil. He squeezes the wet ground, making a ball in his hand. "This is what you wanted, isn't it? This is why you brought me here. To punish me. As if I haven't been punished enough."

He throws the earth bomb and it hits her left shoulder. She's jolted, thrown off balance. She could have easily parried that. *Is he telling the truth? Could it be?*

"What did you think, huh?" he says. "That my parents didn't torment me enough? I was the only one of the four of us who went back to Immaculata, because my father forced me to. Said I had to face the consequences of my actions. My mom doesn't hug me anymore. No one believes that I wasn't responsible for Anne's suicide. And Bobby? And Jordan? And Steve, who was my best friend? They all changed schools, didn't have to deal with the hate that lashed back onto me. Me! Me! And for what, goddammit? Because that basement door was wiiiiide open." His mouth opens wide as he says this. "I was piss drunk. I walked down, for one minute, and because of those cursed sixty seconds, I've had to pay the price until now."

"And you," he adds, a small hump of mossy saliva accumulating at the edge of his mouth. "You crazy bitch-whore-monster. Who do you think you are?"

He makes another earth ball and it almost lands on her

face, missing her by a mere few centimetres. She knows this is a false attack; he's testing her.

She lifts the gun again.

"Enough," she says with tranquil strength.

He rises to his knees and pounds his chest. Screaming. Screaming as loud as he can, like a gorilla or some other ape. He throws his glasses away, into the forest. Can he see without them? she wonders. He begins to punch his face, yelling at the top of his lungs.

"Enough! Stop!"

But he doesn't stop. He continues, harder and harder, until his nose bleeds. Still yelling at the top of his lungs, his voice starts to break.

Judith cannot bear to look at him. She stands and pushes him to the ground to make him stop. Even though he was only kneeling, she is surprised that he actually tips over. He's weaker than she thought.

She is appalled when he attempts to bite her, like an animal. She takes a step back, steadying her position, as her stomach turns and twists with angst. She places her free hand on her belly and breathes deeply, trying to keep the nausea at bay. Her thoughts, like loyal and devoted companions, return to Anne once more. She remembers her daughter's pale face immediately after the photos were posted on Facebook. Remembers the way Anne's thick fingers trembled as she sat at the dining-room table, refusing to eat. Remembers also when, after two days of calling in sick at school, the principal finally called Judith to tell her about the photographs. Will never forget the way Anne cried when she finally told her parents what had happened, refusing to be explicit, refusing to confess any details from that dreadful night with Bobby and the other three boys.

"I want to die," he screams, hitting harder. He begins scratching his chest, making his torso bleed. "I'm sorry! I'm sorry! I'm so fucking sorry she died!"

No, she cannot mentally support this. His actions, words,

her actions, words, weigh heavy. Memories of her daughter, particularly in the weeks leading up to her suicide, agonize and tantalize her. She feels overwhelmed by a sense of generalized regret. She never meant to provoke in Cal what he and his friends had provoked in Anne. It was – it is – all happening so quickly. The duel is taking an unexpected turn; Cal is fighting against himself.

He looks like a vulture-pecked corpse, especially over his chest. His wounds, long scratch lines, are like railways criss-crossing over his rib cage. The blood has yet to dry. His nose still bleeds and his eyes are closed. He looks asleep. His breathing is light. The trench coat has fallen off in the chaos and lies on the ground beside him. She checks his leg. The wound is dark red, not deep. Nothing serious. She feels a sense of relief – he heals fast, the blood has completely dried now.

She sighs deeply. The sun is out, and the wet grass reflects sharp lines of light. She shades her eyes and looks around. They're all alone, still. No birds, nobody, just the tranquil presence of trees.

"Stay here," she says and leaves to go back to the place where they left his clothes. She comes back quickly, pacing and breathing heavily, and feels relieved to find him there. He could have run away to seek help. She lowers his shoes and clothes, which she neatly folded, beside his body.

He opens his lashes slowly, and with the mud and blood, looks like a statue coming to life. "You're back," he says.

"Yes."

He shakes his head. "You want your jacket, is that it?"

She doesn't respond.

"Your phone?"

She had forgotten about her BlackBerry, which is still in the coat pocket.

Very slowly, as if conniving, he slides his arm out from under her trench coat. His knuckles are covered with dry blood. Her chest tightens. Judith is ready for him, is prepared for him to lunge.

He says, "I emailed the recording to myself with a message at the end. If you kill me now, the police will definitely search my inbox for clues. They'll know everything. You're going to jail either way for what you've done." His tone is vindictive. Vicious.

She nods. Yes, he's right. She'll probably end up in jail, no matter what she pleads. Temporary insanity? Spontaneous, unconscious, not pre-meditated. And the way he looks. Battered. They'll blame her for that too, she supposes.

"The gun," he says. "Where is the gun?"

She clutches her purse, unmoving. He understands.

He throws the BlackBerry at her. She catches it and checks the time once again. Three o'clock. She sees all the missed calls and text messages, probably from Shannon or the mayor's office in Montréal. She places the phone into the bag, conscious of the fact that it may be used as evidence against her in court. This fact settles inside of her like a dead weight and she arches her back forward, unaware of the feeling that lowers her head and saddens her features.

So this is the end. She should say something to him. But what? *I'm sorry, you know, I didn't mean to. I lost control.* No. Maybe something more formal. *I'll see you when the legal proceedings begin.* No, that isn't right either. What is there to say, anyway? Nothing. She sighs and turns away.

"Why did you come back?" he asks, suddenly standing up. He crumples her trench coat, wet and bloody, stretches his arm back, aims at her, and then, as if mocking a water-bomb fight, slowly throws it to her. It lands with a slap over her bare arms.

The sight of his blue boxers with their hockey motif disturbs her for the second time that day. This is a child, she thinks, a child.

*Not a child, not as innocent as you think. This is the man that will end your career and could still end your life. Stay on guard.*

His bony body is strong. She can tell by the muscles that flex when he breathes.

"Cat got your tongue?" he asks as his blood-soaked fingers search through his jacket and pants. The pack of cigarettes is soaked. Very carefully, almost tenderly, he searches for one that's dry. He finds one that's damp, broken. He rips it in two, throwing out the tip. After all that effort and care, the lighter won't work. The frustrated look on his face scares her. He screams again, and she opens her purse.

Just in case. In the state he's in, she cannot trust him. The rough grip of her pistol reassures her. This assault will not end on friendly terms, she thinks. They must fight until the end.

She thinks of her daughter again. She wonders what those boys made her go through. Did Bobby force her? Did Cal and the other two threaten her? Or perhaps they just stood there passively – or worse, perversely – entertained by Anne's humiliating position. She does not know, will probably never know the answers to these questions. Yet, whereas before the very questions tortured her mentally, now they merely serve as a mirror, turning to face her. Why did she force the gun into Cal's mouth? Why did she use the pistol to threaten his life? Has she not, at least for a few brief moments, enjoyed his degrading position? Why is she doing this? How painful it is to be in the position of bully, for her at least. How impossible it is to fulfill her fantasy of vengeance by killing Cal. She wants so much to go back in time. She wants to change. Wants to tell Gabriel that she's sorry.

He can tell that she's vulnerable and this changes the look on his face. It deforms his boyish features. He smiles crookedly. "One of us has to die today."

What other consequence could there be of a duel? wonders Judith.

A wet wind hits the back of her neck. The faint smell of fresh grass is beginning to rise from the dark earth around her feet.

He begins to pace around, in tight circles. His muscles are

flexed, as is his jaw. He is clearly angry.

Suddenly, he stops moving. A dreadful panic assaults her. Her breathing is heavy. She breathes through her mouth, which she does not realize is open wide.

The face which was distorted by fury has not slackened. His lips curve and his eyes sparkle with something that instantly renders her terror-stricken.

Fuck. Will she have to kill him?

*No one will believe it was self-defence.*

She takes a step back, keeping her distance.

He wiggles his fingers in the air. Is he provoking her? What is this? She experiences one of those states of being that are like a surrealist painting. She wonders if she is hallucinating, even though she knows this is real. She enters a space inside of her that is dark and void of language. It is a kind of primal fear that freezes her. She is stuck in her unmoving body. If he were to attack her now, she would be completely defenceless.

Instead, he takes off his boxers and throws them over his head. They land on an arched branch and hang there, wet and heavy.

The skin of his penis is dark and crumpled. As if he'd spent the whole day in a warm bath, his testicles have visibly shrunk. His pubic hair is thin and blond.

He squeezes and pulls hard on his penis. The organ bends inside his fist like a beanbag.

*But why is he doing this?*

His gestures become more dramatic, more violent, and she stares, hypnotized by the scene. Tears flow down her face, before she even knows what she's feeling.

Blood rushes to his maltreated organ. It's red, swelling with life. *Why is he doing this?*

Just as his erection begins, he starts to punch his organ. His closed fists slip, land on his pelvic bone, and he continues the aggression.

Her sense of regret is so wide and deep, she worries it will follow her forever, like a dark shadow.

"Stop!"

He looks up at her.

"You have your weapon," he says, licking the saliva that drips from the corner of his mouth. "You have your gun, I have mine." And then, his face changes again. It's as if he's looking at her for the first time. There's something innocent and surprised in his eyes. Like he's saying, "Who are you?" or "Why are you here?"

She takes advantage of this moment of grace. Something like courage, or maybe not, maybe the word is hope, yes, why not, it's hope that gives her the strength to take a semi-step in his direction, lowering the gun ever so slightly.

"Look," she says tentatively. What is it that she wants to tell him? She has no clue what to say. What does one say in these kinds of situations? Look, just relax, let me take you to the hospital? I promise I won't take an exit off the highway, lead you into the forest, and threaten to kill you. The regret. She feels her aura turn black with regret.

"Look," she says again, still uncertain. "You have to stop hating yourself." She bites her lower lip and waits.

He is showing signs of fatigue. He releases his penis, which is pink and white in the places he blocked blood flow.

He lowers his head, lets his penis hang in the air like the tail of a broken clock. Judith thinks he looks possessed.

Her chest is hypersensitive to his every move, as if attuned to him. Breathing hurts. Her neck is swollen and hard. She worries. She worries for his life and her own. His words resonate between her ears, loud and clear: *one of us has to die today.*

When he lifts his head, his eyes are red with tears, filled with agony.

"You," he says, raising his hand in the shape of a gun. The visual impact of his gesture is not lost on her. She is conscious of the hard metal of her SW1911. Wishes for the first time today it wasn't here. Wishes she hadn't pointed the muzzle at him. "You," he says louder. "You've ruined my life."

He laughs a coarse laugh and continues, "You and your goddamn husband. You and your goddamn daughter. *I wish I'd raped her.*"

He stops to look at her. Stops to wait for a reaction. She doesn't blink.

"I had to pay for it," he says. "I paid for it as if I'd raped her. My parents didn't believe me when I told them I'd done nothing. My own father told me he was disgusted by me."

She is touched by this and lets her face show it.

He goes on. "The RCMP was at my place, took my computer. Our neighbours knew. I had to see a shrink for three years. Three years! And my father, my father ..." His voice trails off, but then he swallows and continues. "When I went back to school, the teachers hated me. The guys beat me up at every opportunity for two weeks straight. Everyone knew and no one said a thing. The principal knew but didn't care!"

She nods. She understands.

This gives him the green light to yell. He tilts his head, closing one eye as if aiming at her with his handgun. "And your husband! He went on a crusade. Telling the world that we had raped her! *I* didn't do anything; I didn't do anything to her! When she committed suicide, it was like she'd convicted all of us of sexual assault."

Silence. A chill passes down her back. Her wet clothes stick to her skin uncomfortably. Regret is like a wet cloth, heavy and tenacious. From it drip small drops of sorrow, and one by one, like heart beats, they fall in the depths of her being, dripping and dropping, and echoing painfully in the void. This is not, she thinks, the kind of energy required to win a duel. The emotional abyss makes her wonder whether she will yield. Forfeiting was not a word that had entered her consciousness up until now.

"I had a girlfriend once, you know?" There is something strange in his voice – something both accusatory and pleading. "Two years ago. We met at Carleton. Then, after four months, she calls me crying, asking if it was true. If I was one of the four guys who had raped your daughter. Someone who had gone to our high school and knew Anne told my girlfriend."

They face each other. She, in her wet clothes, holding the gun. He, in his socks, pointing his index finger at her, making the shape of a gun with his hand.

"You hear me? I wish I'd raped her."

His penis hangs between his legs like a dead branch.

She repeats after him, her voice monotone: "You wish you'd raped Anne."

His hand drops. It slaps his thigh and he begins to laugh demonically. Judith cannot keep up with his change of emotions, each one more intense and unexpected than the last. Why is he crying out now as if he were in agony? Truly, thinks Judith, this is a man completely taken by evil spirits, entranced, cursed and consumed by monstrosity.

"I lied," he says, his voice demented. "Anne wasn't a loser with no friends. She was one of the popular girls, very pretty." As he speaks, he lowers his shoulders and his voice changes again. It regains some of its humanity. Judith doesn't trust his face even if his eyes look like open apologies. He bites his nails between sentences. Anne wasn't easy – he doesn't know why he said that. Bobby loved her. Bobby always had girls hanging around him, but not Anne, no.

She raises her gun. Her jaw flexes. And yet, even though she looks as though she's about to advance-lunge, she intuitively knows the battle is over. She hears thunder in her heart. The portrait Cal's now painting of her dead child resonates with her, it reminds her of the Anne she knew and loved, the young woman she had raised.

He avoids her eyes. Anne was the girl that everyone was in love with. But she was disinterested. Never mean. Like a mini-adult, or something, she was way out of everyone's league. That's what pissed off Bobby the most. He had been the group leader since they were in primary school. It was their last year of high school, and she was the only girl he hadn't had.

Judith remembers Anne's first year in high school. She was so dedicated; she had read Shakespeare's *Titus Andronicus* before school had even started. Judith remembers the way Anne's eyes animated when she explained to her parents what she had thought about the play, the ways in which violence was stylized for entertainment. A very pure sorrow settles inside Judith's being. She falls inside of this sadness and continues to fall down the abyss until she hits the hard, flat, crushing pathos of loss. Anne was a brilliant girl. She's gone forever. Hot tears make their silent pilgrimage down Judith's face.

When he looks up at her, the sun hits his blue eyes.

Yes, Anne came to the party with her friends and Bobby had a plan for seducing her. His chest moves up and down quickly.

"Go on," she says, with a crushed tone. Her heart beats in her throat, her ears are hot. Both opponents seem exhausted by the duel.

He runs both hands through his hair. Closes his eyes and says the plan was to seduce her with words. He, Bobby, had learned a poem by some guy called John Donne. They joked about how that would get the job "done."

In what Judith interprets to be a vain tone, Cal recites these lines:

*"Mark but this flea, and mark in this,*
*How little that which thou deniest me is."*

Then, opening his eyes and lowering his voice to a near whisper, he continues:

*"Me it sucked first, and now sucks thee,*
*And in this flea our two bloods mingled be;*

*Thou know'st that this cannot be said*
*A sin, or shame, or loss of maidenhead."*

She looks at him with eyes that could, without doubt, kill. Yes, one of us will die today, she thinks. Then, she releases the safety and rubs the inner skin of her finger against the smooth arc of the trigger.

He starts to jump up and down, arms in the air. It doesn't matter, she thinks, given the distance between them, and even if he moves and tries to attack her, he's dead.

"I didn't know till after," he says. "Jordan's the one who told me. He slipped a ketamine pill in her drink." Unconsciously, Judith shifts her balance, preparing to attack, but before she takes any further action, Cal suddenly stops jumping. Looks at her with pleading eyes. His lungs open and close quickly under his hairless chest.

If only she could see her own face, the way her eyes stare at him with hate and horror. Her nose flaring, Judith's shoulders relax. It's now or never, she thinks. Either she goes for it or she lets it go.

Unaware of Judith's inner battle, Cal goes on, speaking slowly and breathing hard through his flaring nostrils. "I didn't know. I thought she had agreed to go down to the basement with Bobby. I was surprised. When Steve told me he'd seen them go down together, I went down to check. I just couldn't believe it." He kneels down to the ground, supporting his head with his hands. "I went down, and the lights were off except for a lamp and Jordan's cellphone camera. She was barely there, I could tell by the way her eyes were rolling in her head. Steve freaked out right away, told Bobby to stop. Bobby just laughed. Said Steve and I were faggots. Said if we so much as peeped a word to anyone, he'd kill us. We left the basement right away. We left the party a few minutes later."

She takes a step forward and he rolls his arms over his head.

Judith has images of her child's face. She remembers the

Facebook photos, her Anne kneeling in front of Bobby. He wore a blue t-shirt, that's all she can remember. That, and his grin and his black hair. She puts her hand in front of her mouth, suspends her sense of disbelief. Why hadn't Cal told this to the RCMP? How could he have remained silent all this time?

He begins to cry. "I'm sorry," he says. "I'm sorry."

"Do you know what it's like for me to hear you say this?" she asks.

"No. No. Please don't kill me."

"You killed my daughter."

He shakes his head between the armour of his arms. "No, it wasn't me. It wasn't me, it was Bobby and Jordan. We couldn't say anything, *we couldn't*, you understand?"

"No." Her voice is steady. "They hurt her, yes. But that's not what killed her."

He rocks backward and forward.

"What finally killed her was the silence." She waits. Then she adds, "Your silence."

He looks up at her. His bloody, muddy face is twisted with feeling. The gun is not what's causing the pain. He's seen it before; he's been through the threat of death before. It's something else, something new.

"What was I supposed to do?" he asks. But he's not really asking. He's begging for understanding and forgiveness.

"Why didn't you tell the truth?"

He rocks faster.

"I wish I had," he says. "We made a deal. I couldn't rat them out. I couldn't. And then – and then when she killed herself – " He shakes his head, his eyes rolling about in the sockets like marbles. "I knew it was because of us. I knew we were responsible. I wanted to die. I wanted to die." His head hides again under his bony arms.

"Isn't it funny how we unconsciously attract the very situations we are afraid of?" she asks, taking one last step towards him. Her shadow falls across him.

Between sobs, he says, "Tell my mom I love her. I'm sorry. I know I've disappointed her. I'm sorry, oh."

*You have no idea what's going through his mind at this very moment. Whether he's remembering Anne in that dark basement, her mouth full of Bobby. Whether he's remembering your SW1911 in his mouth and the pressure against his tongue, teeth, back of the neck. Maybe he's not thinking about you or your daughter. Maybe he's thinking about his mother, perhaps remembering a time before all this happened, when he was little and she saw him as innocent and good.*

*What did Anne think about before she wrapped a rope around her neck and raised herself on the damn stool; what was going through her mind as she took her last breath? Did she struggle, as the coroner said? Did she want to live after two seconds of choking and regret her decision? You cannot go back on some decisions. They are dead-ends, definitive, fatal.*

*Would you have regrets and be filled with demons, the way Cal is, if you pulled the trigger? Would you live the rest of your life with remorse – could you? How? To be imprisoned like an animal, not just physically but psychically jailed? Would it be worth it to take Cal's life, and what would it bring you? Would you finally have the peace you've craved since Anne's death? No, of course not. Vengeance is a meal you eat cold, without pleasure or satisfaction. It would mean forfeiting your humanity and this, to sense your humanity, the aliveness, the life within you, is what you have most wanted since Anne's suicide.*

# Seven

The sun lets its light flow down to earth like a waterfall, gushing and splashing over the grass and leaves. He realizes he is still alive when he hears the sound of leaves brushing against each other, flies buzzing nearby and the cricket chorus that previously disappeared in the background of his mind. Time has passed. And he is alive. The last thing he remembers before blacking out is a painful shock on the side of his head. He touches it now and feels a bump. She must have hit him with the pistol and knocked him out.

He emerges from his crouched body as a soldier emerging from battle, shocked and perplexed at the silence. As if suspecting it of hiding something. Standing, he looks around with wild eyes. A branch snaps behind him and he jumps up. False alarm. A chipmunk or a bird, maybe. He feels watched. As if someone is toying with him.

"Are you here?" he asks. "Show yourself. Don't play with me. Just kill me."

He opens his arms wide. "Just put me out of my misery already," he says.

Minutes pass. The sky is blue. Small colonies of clouds have their backs turned to him in the distance. Suddenly, he *knows* she is gone. She has spared him.

A tiny grey fox pokes its head out from a shrub with wide, waxy leaves. It stares at him a moment, with shiny dark eyes, and then puts one paw forward. Soon, it emerges from the bush, its ash fur glistening. It hops over a fallen branch, and trots past him before disappearing again into the bush.

He looks up at the sky and then, blinded by the light, closes his eyes. He says, "Thank you," to the sky. He does not believe in a god or disbelieve in one. He used to go to Sunday mass with his parents when he was little, but after Immaculata, lost all faith in organized religion. Lost faith in a good and beneficent higher consciousness. Now, however, he senses a presence. A warm and brilliant light within him and all around him. Experiences like these have a way of bringing one closer to higher powers. He knows it's irrational and folly to think this, but he believes in that moment that God must have intervened on his behalf.

As he puts his boxers back on, he considers Judith.

If he were her, he would have killed him. No doubt about it.

He wants to dry his clothes on tree branches but is compelled to put them on and leave as quickly as possible. It doesn't feel safe here. He turns in circles for some time before finding the pathway that leads to the parking lot. Her car is gone. There are two trucks parked at opposite ends, a white and a blue one. He runs to the blue one first, trying to open the door. Nothing, the truck is empty. The same thing with the second. He hits the door in frustration. He runs back to the path and yells out for someone, anyone. No answer. No telephone booth. His cellphone is in his bag, which is probably still in her car, along with his wallet, which holds his driver's license and health card, his money.

He walks to the highway. Cars zoom by him. He sees a woman with short brown hair and large glasses point at him. He knows she can see him, and yet the white Volkswagen drives past him. Determined, he tries to flag a car down. He even jumps up and waves as a large truck passes him by, but no luck. Frustrated, he walks onward, toward the gas station. If his memory serves him right, they passed one just before exiting the highway.

The blue oval and the red font of the Esso station sign almost make him want to weep. How beautiful, this advertisement. It confirms he is safe. He is safe.

It takes all the strength he has to walk two hundred metres to the station. His chest aches and stings. His back is hunched over and he has begun to limp. Though not serious, the scar on his leg hurts. An intense desire to sleep overwhelms him.

When he opens the door, the air conditioning stings him like an electrical shock. The girl at the counter looks appalled. Behind her hangs a small television, and he sees his whole body reflected on the screen. Wet, with a suit that hangs loose over him, his face bloody and black with soil, he looks like he's been abducted by aliens and brought back to earth.

His shoes are sloshing and he leaves a trail of water as he advances toward the counter.

"Can I help you?" she says, her head leaning back, her mouth twisted with disgust.

"Yes. Please. I need help."

She is beautiful, with long blonde hair. It's wavy and goes past her shoulders. Her eyes are dark brown, and her long lashes flutter in a mixture of fear and admiration. She looks like she's in her early twenties. He is aware of his body, aware of the way he must look, like a madman. And yet, somehow, he smiles at her with genuine good feeling and miraculously, she abandons the dreadful look on her face and smiles back. He knows he must call his parents. He knows, too, that he must call the RCMP. He owes it to Anne and most of all, he owes it to Judith. She who spared him and gave him a second chance at life, for her sake if not for his own, he would redeem himself.

She doesn't know. She doesn't know who or what aspect of her being could have so brutally abused that boy. She sits in the car, rubbing her forehead, rubbing it hard as if trying to erase a stain. She is but one exit past the place where she pointed the gun to his face. This gun that he choked on while she played out her revenge fantasy, completely unaware of the damage she was inflicting upon him. And upon herself, for that matter. And yet, there is an inexplicable simplicity of being right now that she hasn't experienced since Anne's death; a kind of release which brings her inner clarity and freedom. She wants to cry and laugh, but doesn't have the will or energy for either.

Exit Number 88. She is in an abandoned parking lot for what used to be a fast food restaurant called "Debra's." The wooden banner hangs to the left, and the black paint has suffered many seasons, she can tell by the way the paint fades off the letters 'e,' 'b' and 'a'. Everything fades, she thinks, even the letters in our first names. And yet, strangely, her identity feels grounded. Solid.

She looks at the concrete walls of the empty restaurant. Architecture is above all a visual sense, with less emphasis placed on other faculties of perception. The location of this building, however, in the middle of nowhere, demands special consideration of the auditory sense. There is no sound here but the engines of the cars that pass by on the highway parallel to the main road. The concrete walls, painted white and chipped at the edges, clearly act as vaults, shielding the property both visually and acoustically from the character of the highway.

Her body feels as solid and as raw as the restaurant walls. She is ready to assume responsibility for what she has done.

Regret feels real to her, like an organ pulsing with life. Maybe it's in her skin, covering the entire frame of her being. The sense of total loss was like a tipping point. Behind the peak of her remorse lies the possibility of something new. But what?

She shakes her head. It's going to take her a long time to integrate the complexity of what has happened today, she knows. All of the dualistic voices within her seem to be resting now. She has no doubt that she has committed a great crime against Cal. She has no doubt that Anne would not have wanted it to be like this.

Again, she shakes her head.

The view in front of her is splendid. There is a rainbow that arches above the highway, over Debra's, and past the corn field in the back of the main road. She finds the colours subtle and stunning.

Why did she have to almost kill someone to be reminded that colours are beautiful? Why did she have to commit such an extreme act of violence to finally see what is right in front of her? To see things as they are. Simply as they are.

Anne is dead. She will never come back. The loss will stay with her always like her eyes between the sack of bones that hold them in place.

And the regret, the regret. Oh, the regret. If only she had acted more consciously. If only she hadn't followed him into the forest. The gun. She looks at her purse resting on the passenger's side. There, she notices Cal's bag under the glove compartment. She closes her eyes momentarily before opening her bag, which is still wet from the rain. The SW1911 looks the same as it did earlier that day, when she first found it in her bedroom. It looks the same as it did yesterday and the week before at shooting practice.

The wind is gentle. Her arms react to the breeze with goosebumps. She walks into the empty field in front of Debra's, filled with daffodils and clovers. She tries not to step on them as she walks toward the highway. What is the Latin name of daffodils again? she wonders. Cal would know if he were here.

The gun is close to her outer thigh. She stops halfway down the field and throws it on the bright green grass. Then, she kneels down and rips the grass with her bare hands. She is surprised at how easy it is to invade the wet soil. She throws a few small rocks to the side. As she works, she looks up to see a white car zoom by, followed by a large truck. When she is done digging the hole with her fingers, she drops the SW1911 and covers it up.

She removes a strand of hair from her face and a line of soil covers her forehead. She can smell the earth and grass and smiles as she walks back to the car. She experiences a strange feeling of satisfaction after having concealed the gun, as if she had buried her daughter for the second time. Then, she sees a blackbird land on the roof of her car. Here is your omen of bad things to come, thinks Judith. Or maybe not: blackbirds were friends of her daughter's – she remembers once more how they brought Anne gifts of gratitude – is this one a messenger from the other world? The bird chirps merrily and flies off, over the highway and into the horizon. Judith laughs at her own thought process. Still, she wonders, for reasons she cannot explain, if the blackbird isn't foreshadowing something good. Getting back into the car, she knows that she will have to pay whatever consequences are imposed on her by the rule of law for what she has done to the boy. Yes, she knows that it will never take away the despicable and inhumane atrocities she has committed. Jail or no jail, she will forever bear the burden of the loss of her daughter and her attack on Cal. Nonetheless, she feels liberated.

*The Ottawa Magazine*
*December 11, 2016*

## CITY ART INSIDER: Dumont-Belović Duo To Open The Ottawa Art Factory

*Ottawa Magazine* stops by to visit Gabriel Dumont and Judith Belović as they oversee the final weeks of renovations ahead of the opening of The Ottawa Art Factory, a stone's throw away from the National Art Gallery.

Last time we tried to interview the couple together, Belović did not show up, and Dumont gave an evocative plea for justice for his daughter who had been allegedly sexually abused by four boys from her high school. She was subsequently bullied, dropped out of high school and eventually committed suicide. The news shocked the whole nation in 2011, prompting the federal government to pass anti-bullying and anti-cyberbullying laws.

The traumatic events precipitated the divorce between the award-winning author and celebrated architect. That was four years ago and much has changed since then.

Most shocking was the surprising conviction last summer of two of the four boys who had been let go free of charge by the RCMP four years ago. We have not questioned the couple on any of this, as per our agreement before coming to interview them about the Art Factory. Nonetheless, we couldn't help but wonder if that had anything to do with their reconciliation.

"We remarried in the fall," says Dumont, beaming. He touches his white-gold ring as he tells the story of how the two "fell in love for the second time."

Beside him, Belović sits and smiles, obviously touched, obviously a woman in love with her husband, a woman slowly coming to terms with a terrible loss.

"There are those who experience loss, lose their minds, their spirit and let everything that is sacred inside of them die. They get divorced. They don't believe in relationships. This is a kind of death," says Dumont. "There are those who fall to the ground after trauma and stay there, almost crippled, until one day the river swells with spring and they begin to smell flowers once again. When you get your sense of smell back, you begin to savour life again. It's that simple."

Belović shakes her head. "Gabriel is sentimental," she says. "Verging on the edge of clichéd, sometimes."

They look at each other and laugh. They share a kind of complicity that you'd expect of a twenty-year old couple, not a once-married and then remarried couple who have survived the loss of their only child.

When asked if they consider themselves healed, especially given the recent convictions of two of the four boys, their faces retain only a fraction of the lustre that shone a minute ago. "Healing," says Belović in a sober voice, "is a process. You do not heal and move forward unscathed. You are continuously healing. The past persists."

Dumont points to the vase beside them. It's light blue and was visibly cracked and then glued back together with gold.

Belović explains the piece is part of the opening exhibition the two have curated for the opening of the Art Factory. The opening exhibition, enigmatically titled *Kintsukuroi*, will open in mid-March.

"Kintsukuroi," says Belović, "is the Japanese art of repairing pottery with gold or silver lacquer and understanding that the piece is more beautiful for having been broken."

The couple is visibly proud to open Ottawa's first Art Factory, located in the heart of the Market.

Belović sold her architecture firm in the middle of the summer and bought an old building at the corner of Parent and St. Patrick, which she then destroyed in order to create the stunning structure that will welcome artists of all genres as of next summer. The simplest way to describe it is to say it looks like a beehive from the outside and a labyrinth on the inside.

Made of vertical and horizontal fins and slats built from recycled pine wood and timber, the venue has a distinctive profile inspired by the tiny insects' home. It incorporates other green materials, such as poplar, to blend harmoniously with the pine and timber. Held together by used utility poles with yellow stain, the structure seems as if it's been reclaimed from a distant childhood memory. It aims to give homage to nature while creating an extraordinary experience that will inspire artists to create other edgy and experimental works.

"Yes, that's about right," says Belović, visibly pleased by our description. "A natural beehive is an architectural splendour." She stops and closes her eyes, as if remembering something or someone. She smiles and then continues, "Its dome structure is very interesting."

"Honeycomb cells are symmetrical and we wanted to have lots of light coming into the building, so we made each cell into a window," she says, her voice becoming a whisper. "It was a challenge."

Dumont adds that they love the figurative value of the beehive, because bees are social creatures that collaborate together to make something sweet. The pun, though an obvious one, makes us all laugh.

But why the maze-like atmosphere inside the building? Once you enter the beehive, you arrive in an empty oval room with concrete walls. Seven columns surround you and lead to seven doors, except for the enormous set of round stairs in the middle that lead to the rooftop. Each door leads to a unique room with an eccentric design. One of them is completely black. There is no light that enters the room, as the windows have been painted black.

"It's the childhood room," says Dumont. "It shows the blackout memories, the ones that leave us with a sense of dread." He has painted some chilling verse on the walls:

Line of sight, line of thought, lifeline

In the beginning, the wrong turn
In the pivot point of misfortune
In the falling apart of a thought
In the end, nothing remains but the remains

The gaps, the accidents, the fissures that line the wall

When asked if this room has anything to do with his daughter, Dumont is elusive. Belović says all houses have black rooms, some of us are simply not aware of it. Their faces, when probed about the childhood room, become as rigid as two planks of wood.

We are allowed to see only one other room, room number five. Through a set of red and white wooden doors with a chequered pattern and big brass handles, visitors enter into a complex and inexplicable design. The hardwood floor is a pale grey, rustic in style. From it emerge sharp glass shreds, about a metre or two in height, that are arranged in a maze-like fashion. From the ceiling, more sharp glass shreds hang dangerously, like swords. Belović, completely unaffected by our reaction, assures us it's safe. It is Plexiglas mixed with plastic, held in place by industrial-sized steel bolts. They call this the "Silent Room," but the other visitors and I agree: it makes us want to scream.

Between the hanging Plexiglas are large drawings of an Asian woman sitting, a pair of scissors on the floor beside her. In another drawing, a man is cutting a piece of her clothing. These scenes are quite disturbing, especially in the context of the shards of glass, which feel threatening. What makes it even more daunting are the sound recordings of a woman's voice whispering the words "Who am I?" and "What have I done?"

"Yoko Ono" is all Belović will say to us. "Drawings by Argentinian street artist Andandor." When we ask what the link between silence and violence is, Belović appears annoyed by our question. "That seems obvious," she says, while Dumont appears to agree with her.

We ask her about the voice recording, if it is her speaking, and not surprisingly, she merely shakes her head and says nothing.

It is obvious to us that the two rooms were choreographed and linked by a personal vision which, like two pieces of conceptually different puzzles, are not meant to fit perfectly together. Instead, they echo each other through space and time, like two memories that are linked but not necessarily related. When asked if this interpretation resonates with her, Belović says we are better off resisting interpretation. "It usually leads one away from the immediate experience of things and into some other space inside our heads."

"We aimed to create a space where artists could experiment freely and be themselves. Without constraints. We've already had a number of high-profile artists ask us when they can start working here," says Dumont.

Belović says a committee of judges will decide who can create here, and for how long. The criteria will be based entirely on artistic merit, quality of work and strength of vision.

As we leave the future art gallery, we are reminded of the powerful aura of this cultural power couple, and cannot wait to come back for the opening of *Kintsukuroi* in mid-March. While we have no doubt the exhibition will be welcomed by artists and public alike, we are sure the most chilling and amazing aspect will be the building itself. That and, of course, the two creative minds behind it, Belović and Dumont.

# ACKNOWLEDGEMENTS

Anne Cunningham, my dear editor: thank you for your invaluable encouragement, feedback and care. It made the process of writing a pleasure.

Thank you to Joanna Reid for your insight and editorial feedback – your support over the last few years has made me grow as a writer. I would also like to extend my gratitude to Marie-Pierre Daigle for her support, patience and love during the writing of *Psychomachia*. My brother, Ismar Fejzić, who has always believed in my work and me deserves a special mention. Thank you for your enthusiasm and generosity of spirit, little brother. Merci beaucoup Mathieu Laca pour ton support et ton amitié. Finally, I am grateful and indebted to my parents, extended family, teachers and all of the friends and colleagues that have entered my life and forever changed it with their presence.

To Luciano Iacobelli and Allan Briesmaster: thank you for championing the novella in Canada.

**Other Recent Quattro Fiction**

*The Other Oscar* by Cora Siré
*Blackbird Calling* by Laura Swart
*Travel Is So Broadening* by Wasela Hiyate
*Tomas and the Gypsy Violin* by Robert Eisenberg
*Escape!!!* by J.P. Rodriguez
*Loopholes* by Showey Yazdanian
*The Escape Artist* by Anita Kushwaha
*Too Much on the Inside* by Danila Botha
*The Duck Lake Chronicles* by John C. Goodman
*An Imperfect Man* by John Calabro
*JAZZ* by Elizabeth Copeland
*The Green Hotel* by Jesse Gilmour
*Down the Street* by Cassandra Cronenberg
*Costume & Bone* by Lucinda Johnston
*The Girl Before, the Girl After* by Louis-Philippe Hébert
*Rough Paradise* by Alec Butler
*Look at Me* by Robert Shoub
*Dempsey's Lodge* by Eric Wright
*Inheritance* by Kirsten Gundlack
*Oatcakes and Courage* by Joyce Grant-Smith
*Terminal Grill* by Rosemary Aubert
*World of Glass* by Jocelyne Dubois
*The Sandbar* by Jean-Paul Daoust
*Texas* by Claudio Gaudio
*Abundance of the Infinite* by Christopher Canniff
*The Proxy Bride* by Terri Favro
*Tea with the Tiger* by Nathan Unsworth
*A Certain Grace* by Binnie Brennan
*Life Without* by Ken Klonsky
*Romancing the Buzzard* by Leah Murray
*The Lebanese Dishwasher* by Sonia Saikaley
*Against God* by Patrick Senécal
*The Ballad of Martin B.* by Michael Mirolla
*Mahler's Lament* by Deborah Kirshner